"One yell," Clayburn whispered, "and you're a dead general."

Otero blinked at him stupidly. He looked down at the gun; at Clayburn's thumb on the hammer, ready to cock it back.

When he looked up at Clayburn again his eyes were narrow, and not at all stupid. "Think well, Captain. . . . Whatever you intend, you cannot possibly get away alive afterwards."

"You'll make sure I *do* get away alive," Clayburn told him. "This commits me. From here on, no matter what I do or don't do, I'll be killed if I'm caught. So it can't possibly go any worse for me if I kill you first. And if you do anything—anything at all—to help me get caught, I *will* kill you. Be very sure of that."

THREE RODE NORTH

Marvin H. Albert

FAWCETT GOLD MEDAL · NEW YORK

A Fawcett Gold Medal Book
Published by Ballantine Books
Copyright © 1964 by Al Conroy

ISBN 0-449-13384-2

Manufactured in the United States of America

First Ballantine Books Edition: January 1990

ONE

Terror stabbed through Domaso Vari's guts like a knife of ice when he saw the riders coming over the crest of the hill toward him. He rose from the small fire over which he was preparing his mid-day meal and watched them ride down into the tiny spring-fed valley where his seven sheep grazed.

Twenty mounted men, all armed with pistols and rifles.

Domaso held himself very still, making no move that might be interpreted to mean that he had something special to fear from them. And he did not. Of all men in Mexico, he had least to do with anything that might anger these riders. Politics were no part of his world. He was a poor shepherd; nothing else.

He was afraid now only because they were what they were. Something to be feared. Like a scorpion. Or a trembling volcano.

They were General Otero's troops, though they wore no uniform. No one else was permitted to have weapons in the part of northern Sonora over which Otero had seized control. Everyone had been ordered to turn over any arms they had to the new authorities. Villages where some had been caught trying to hide guns had been burned, all their people slaughtered—as a warning.

The mounted men approached across the grassy level past the sheep, riding slowly, two men in the lead studying the ground as they rode. Now Domaso saw that most of them were not Mexicans, and the cold knife of fear inside him twisted deeper.

1

These were the ones known as The Foreigners; though it was true some of them were Mexican. Renegade killers from many lands, led by a man called Dietrich. The cutting edge of Otero's army, it was said, chiefly responsible for Otero's victories. Some even said it was now the man called Dietrich who ruled; that General Otero seldom came out of his fortress to be seen any more, having become Dietrich's puppet.

Domaso didn't know if this was true, and didn't care. He knew nothing, wanted to know nothing. . . . Pulling off his wide-brimmed straw hat he held it in both hands in front of him, a short, squat, humble figure waiting as the jaws of fate closed on him.

They drew rein in a circle around him. About a dozen of them dismounted, some moving to stand close behind Domaso. One of those who did not dismount was obviously their leader—a strongly-built man with a coldly aristocratic face. Domaso had never seen Dietrich before, but he'd heard him described. A face like a blond devil, they said. The description fit.

Dietrich sat erect in his saddle and watched as a thin man named Hogan, his best tracker, studied the ground around the fire for a few moments. Hogan rode slowly away up the north slope, studying the ground all the way. Atop the crest he drew rein, gazing off into the distance through a pair of fieldglasses. Then he put the glasses away and rode back down to Dietrich.

"He was here sometime this morning. Stayed a while, let his horse graze. Then rode on still going north. Across that desert. Far enough ahead for the wind to've already covered his tracks with sand."

Dietrich nodded, leaned forward with both hands on his saddle horn, and looked down at Domaso. There was no cruelty in his bright blue eyes, as there was in some of the other eyes that were watching the shepherd. But there was something much worse: a total lack of recognition of Domaso as a fellow human, even one to be scorned. Dietrich looked down at Domaso as though he were a faintly interesting bug.

"Where is Juan Ramirez going?" Dietrich's Spanish was good, but with a harsh accent, unpleasant to the ear.

Domaso had never heard of Juan Ramirez. But he understood now what kind of trouble he was in. "I do not know," he stuttered. "I know no man with such a name." A hand seemed to be gripping his throat, strangling him, making each word hard to force out.

"He was here with you this morning," Dietrich said.

"A man *was* here," Domaso agreed hastily, feeling the sudden sweat drenching his ragged clothes. "He did not tell me his name. He rode in at dawn. I shared my meal with him and filled his canteen before he rode on. It was only hospitality. But if I should not have, I am sorry. I did not know. . . ."

"Where did he ride?"

"North."

"North I know," Dietrich said patiently. "Where north?"

Domaso shrugged helplessly, clenching his hat tightly with both hands. "I do not know. He did not say."

It was possible, Dietrich recognized, that the shepherd spoke the truth. That he didn't know the man who'd shared his breakfast, didn't know where he was going, and had never even heard of Juan Ramirez. Most of the peasants of this country would not yet know the name of the leader of the opposition to General Otero.

It was possible. But Dietrich preferred to be certain. And there was only one way to be certain.

He made a motion with one hand. Two of the men behind Domaso seized the shepherd's arms, twisting them behind him. Domaso did not resist, knowing it was useless. He stared wide-eyed at the huge, powerful-looking man who dismounted and came toward him, a cruel smile on his dark, brutal face.

This man's name was Morales, and he was the strongest man among those who followed Dietrich. He drew leather gloves on his big hands and smiled into Domaso's face and asked: "Where is Juan Ramirez going?"

Domaso felt his legs go watery and his heart thudding inside his ribs like a trip-hammer. "I do not know!" he bleated. "I swear before God I do not. . . ."

Morales spread his feet for balance and drove a fist deep into the pit of the shepherd's stomach, twisting his massive shoulders behind the blow. The sound that burst out of Domaso's wide-open mouth was scarcely human. His legs collapsed under him and he sagged, retching, in the grip of the two men who held him up by his arms.

Morales drove three more such blows into Domaso's middle before he stepped back and looked up at Dietrich. "He has fainted."

"Wake him," Dietrich ordered calmly.

Morales got Domaso's water bag and opened it. Grasping the shepherd's hair to raise his head, he poured water on his unconscious face. Domaso came awake sputtering and moaning, blood welling up in his mouth and trickling down his lip. His legs moved weakly, aimlessly, as his eyes tried to focus.

"Where is Juan Ramirez going?" Dietrich repeated.

"Please . . . !" Domaso gasped. ". . . for the love of God . . . I do not know. . . ."

Dietrich moved his head in a small, single nod. Morales went back to work, on the shepherd's face this time. His first punch smashed Domaso's nose. The second and third were flush on the mouth, snapping off teeth. Morales went on with it, enjoying himself, alternating between the face and stomach.

Dietrich turned his horse and rode up the north slope. He was fairly sure now that the shepherd did not know anything. But he gave no orders for Morales to stop what he was doing. To be absolutely certain, something like that had to be carried through to its conclusion.

Hogan followed Dietrich to the top of the slope and the two gazed together out over the desert stretching to the north.

After a moment, Hogan said, "My guess'd be he's heading across the border into Arizona."

"That's a safe guess." Dietrich's English was better than his Spanish, the Germanic accent slight. "The question is why. For guns . . . or men . . . or . . . ?"

"Could be he's just calling it quits. Getting out while he still can."

Dietrich shook his head. "Juan Ramirez won't quit. Men like him have to be killed to be stopped."

He continued to stare north. Wherever Juan Ramirez was

going, and for whatever reason, he'd almost certainly pass through one of the towns just north of the border. He'd be in need of supplies, food. . . .

From this point he would most likely be heading for one of three towns: Nogales, Douglas, or Tubavi Springs.

Dietrich stayed there on the crest for some time, thinking about it. Finally he turned his horse and rode back down into the little valley, with Hogan trailing him.

Domaso was sprawled on the ground, unconscious. There wasn't enough left of the shepherd's face for anyone to recognize him by. Just torn flesh and broken bones. He was still breathing, but weakly, erratically. Morales poured the rest of the water from the pigskin bag on the bloody remains of Domaso's features, with no result. He raised a leg and drove his bootheel into Domaso's side, viciously. There was no more response from Domaso than if he'd been a sack of grain.

Morales looked up at Dietrich and shrugged. "It will be a long time before this one comes to again. If ever."

Dietrich nodded and looked sideways at Hogan. "Want to try that draw again?" He looked at another of his men. "Call it."

Hogan poised his right hand over his holstered gun, his eyes narrowed on the unconscious figure of the shepherd on the ground. Morales quickly stepped back out of the way. Dietrich made no move at all, both hands resting on his saddle horn.

"Now!" the caller snapped.

Then Dietrich's hand moved and his Colt was in his hand, the flat, harsh report of the shot beating against the slopes, the bullet hammering into Domaso's forehead a split-second before Hogan's ripped into the shepherd's chest.

A mounted man laughed. Hogan's pride in his speed was known to all of them; and his ability to beat any of them to the draw—except Dietrich. Hogan, the gun still in his hand, twisted toward the man. The laughter ceased abruptly.

A faint smile touched the corners of Dietrich's mouth as he holstered his gun and gave his orders. Minutes later they were all gone from the little valley, leaving it to the grazing sheep and the smoldering coals of the fire and the sprawled, motionless body of Domaso Vari.

Most of the mounted killers rode back south from the valley with Dietrich. But three went north, hunting for Juan Ramirez.

One headed for Nogales. The second angled away towards Douglas.

Hogan rode north to Tubavi Springs.

Six nights later in Tubavi Springs, a gambler named Clayburn sat at a poker table losing steadily because his mind was not entirely on the game.

He kept wondering when the hell Juan Ramirez was going to show up. . . .

"How many?"

Clayburn wrenched his mind back to his hand. Two aces, two queens, and a five of spades. He discarded the five. The dealer beside him flipped him a single card and flipped cards to the other players. Clayburn's long, lean fingers eased the card into his hand. Another queen. He looked at the money he had left in front of him. Sixty dollars.

"Bet them or fold them," the dealer said.

Clayburn bet his last sixty dollars on the two aces and three queens. The others around the poker table slowly folded their cards. Except for a tough, ruddy-faced cattleman across from him. He eyed Clayburn, eyed his hand, and pushed sixty dollars into the pot.

"See you."

Clayburn spread his cards face-up on the table. "Full house."

The cattleman beamed and showed his cards. "Read 'em and weep, gambler."

Clayburn looked at the four jacks in the cattleman's hand. There was a hard shine to his narrowed green eyes. His lean, weathered, strong-boned face got a mildly disgusted set to it. He stood up, took a black, flat-crowned hat off the back of his chair, and put it on his head.

He was a tall, lanky man with heavy sloping shoulders, dressed in black except for a gold cravat and the bone handle of the gun holstered low on his right hip. A man with a stubborn, sardonic mouth and a lazy coiled-spring way of moving.

"Wiped out?" one of the other men in the game asked.

"Just about."

The cattleman laughed. "Nothing I like better'n trimming a professional."

"Glad you enjoyed it," Clayburn was angry. Not at the cattleman. With himself. He didn't like to lose and he didn't blame his losing on bad luck. Gambling required patient concentration. On the other players as well as on the cards.

If he'd been concentrating he wouldn't have thrown away the sixty dollars. The cattleman had kept three cards. When he'd looked at the two he'd drawn, he had flexed his left shoulder a little. Clayburn remembered now, that the cattleman had flexed his shoulder like that a number of times previous during the evening's play. And each time it had turned out that he'd improved his hand. If Clayburn had been paying attention he would have noted it sooner, and realized the cattleman had built three of a kind into four of a kind.

"If you can borrow another stake," the cattleman said expansively, "you're always welcome back in the game."

"I'll be back," Clayburn told him. He didn't like to lose. He turned away from the table and started across the room.

The gambling room behind the saloon was crowded. Tubavi Springs was just north of the border, on a route used by cattle trailers, freight lines and mustangers moving back and forth between Mexico and Arizona. And this was the only gambling place in town.

Clayburn pushed past the dice tables and the faro game and went out into the main part of the saloon.

A man nursing a whiskey at the bar watched Clayburn cross the room. He did it without turning, his pale lusterless eyes following Clayburn in the mirror behind the bar. He was a thin rail of a man with long skinny hands, straight sandy hair and a tense, sharp-featured face.

His name was Hogan.

He waited until Clayburn went out through the saloon door. Then he put down his half-finished drink and followed.

TWO

Going outside into the dry heat of the night air, Hogan stood for a moment against the adobe wall of the saloon, gazing after the figure of Clayburn moving off through the dark-shadowed street.

Juan Ramirez had come to Tubavi Springs. But he'd been gone by the time Hogan had arrived. General Otero had a spy living in Tubavi Springs and he'd been keeping an eye on the owner of a restaurant in the Mexican section of town; a man suspected of being in contact with the rebels south of the border. According to the spy, Juan Ramirez had spent a night catching up with his sleep in a room over the Mexican restaurant, then had ridden on north at dawn.

Hogan had tried to find Juan Ramirez's trail out of town, without success. He'd been about to head back south when Otero's spy had come to him with another piece of information. A gambler named Clayburn had gotten off the stage and gone straight to the Mexican restaurant. After a private talk with the owner, Manuel Santos, the gambler had moved into the same room over the restaurant that Juan Ramirez had used.

This was strange, for the gambler was a gringo, and Manuel Santos did not rent that room to strangers. It could be that this Clayburn had some business with the rebels south of the border.

It was more than possible, Hogan had agreed. He'd gone to have a look at Clayburn, and decided he had the look of a fighting man more than a gambler. There was always a chance, Hogan had decided, that this man would head south and lead him to the rebels. Or even that Juan Ramirez would return to Tubavi Springs, and that Clayburn was here waiting for him. The possibility was strong enough to keep Hogan in town a while longer, waiting and watching.

So far he'd waited three days since Clayburn had shown up. Alternately watching Clayburn and the owner of the restaurant. But mostly Clayburn. . . .

Now Hogan waited until Clayburn was far enough away down the dark, dusty street. Then he started after him, keeping his distance, looking like another of the many trail hands using the hard dirt streets that night. Hogan knew how to trail a man without being caught at it. A man hunter who couldn't do that died young. And Hogan was still alive after some six years of making a hazardous living at it. . . .

Clayburn turned into a long alley that led behind the squat adobe building that housed the Mexican restaurant. There was no brass candle-holder in the small side window. Which meant that Juan still hadn't returned.

Clayburn had been in Wyoming when the message from Juan Ramirez had finally caught up with him—a month after it had been sent. The message had asked him to come here and see the owner of a Mexican restaurant, Manuel Santos. It didn't explain why, beyond the fact that Juan needed him. Which was explanation enough. Clayburn had come by the shortest train and stage routes south.

Manuel Santos had been guarded with Clayburn, not knowing him or what his relationship was to the Ramirez family. He claimed not to know where Juan Ramirez was, and told Clayburn only what he'd been instructed to say.

Juan Ramirez had come through Tubavi Springs one night six weeks ago, and had told Manuel to expect a man named Clayburn. When Clayburn came, he was to tell him to wait until he was contacted. Twice since then a man had come from Juan to ask for Clayburn. Then, only two days before Clayburn arrived, Juan had re-appeared. He had asked for Clayburn, and had appeared disappointed to learn that Clayburn had never come. Then he had gone away. But he would be back. When, the restaurant owner did not know.

Clayburn had said he'd wait, and Manuel had put him up in the little spare room over the restaurant. But though Clayburn had probed for more information about Juan—and his father, Diego—Manuel would tell him nothing further about what was going on.

Clayburn could guess at some of it. As he'd come south into Arizona he'd begun to hear about a Mexican politician now calling himself General Otero, who'd gotten control of part of northern Sonora. A damned harsh control. And he was presently engaged in slaughtering the opposition to his rule. Since the Ramirez ranch was located in that section of Sonora, it didn't take much thinking to figure out that Diego and his son were somehow mixed up with Otero's opposition.

Abruptly, as he reached the end of the alley, Clayburn forced these thoughts out of his mind. Juan would show up when he'd show up, and explain everything. Until then, he had time to recoup his poker losses. And that was all he intended to occupy his mind with for the remainder of this night.

He opened the rear door of the building and stepped into a narrow hall behind the kitchen. The sounds and spicy odors of the restaurant reached him as he climbed a short flight of wooden steps to his room. Getting out a key, he unlocked the door and took one step inside.

There was a sound of someone breathing, just to his left in the darkness of the room.

Clayburn slammed the door shut behind him so that he was no longer outlined in the faint lamplight from the stairway. In a continuation of the same movement he twisted to the left, rammed into someone, and grabbed with both hands.

His strong fingers closed on plump, vibrant flesh that was distinctly female. There was a gasp of pain that was also distinctly female. The pointed toe of a hard boot cracked against his shin.

Clayburn made a small sound in his throat, slid his hands down the struggling woman's arms to her hands. There was a knife in her unseen right hand. His fingers tightened around her wrist, twisting viciously. She let out another gasp, and the knife clattered on the floor. He continued to twist until he had her turned around, her back to him and her left wrist shoved up between her shoulder blades.

Still she didn't scream out loud. She cursed, fervently and fluently in Spanish; but softly, whispering the curses through tight-clenched teeth. Clayburn held her with one hand and marched her forward until she collided with the bureau. Digging a match from his pocket with his free hand, he snapped it alight with his thumbnail and lit the kerosene lamp on the bureau. Then he let go of her.

She spun around to face him, breathing hard, not trying to slide away. She wore a man's shirt and Levi's on a lean, taut figure that looked as vibrant as it had felt. Straight pitch-black hair framed a striking, sensual face—dark eyes that flared over high, bold cheekbones; a short, strong nose; lips that made Clayburn think of rich ripe fruit waiting to be bitten into and tasted.

"What's your name?" she demanded harshly, in English flavored with a Mexican accent.

He told her his name.

She relaxed a bit, unclenching her fists and rubbing her wrist. "You hurt me." It wasn't a complaint; merely a stated fact.

"You shouldn't come at a man with a knife."

"I was afraid you might be a spy . . . I'm glad I didn't kill you."

A corner of Clayburn's sardonic mouth quirked. "I'm glad I didn't let you."

She sneered at him. "Let me? If I had wanted to, I would have put the knife between your ribs instead of kicking you."

Clayburn smiled, enjoying her. His greenish eyes traveled slowly down her taut, vibrant figure and up again, a familiar itch starting in the palms of his hands and spreading outward. She caught her breath as though it were his fingers moving over her. Then her lips curved a little, and her eyes narrowed on him, studying him. Faintly interested, faintly amused, very sure of herself.

"My name is Serina," she told him, her voice richer and

deeper than it had been before. "Manuel says you wait for Juan Ramirez."

"What are you doing in here?" Clayburn asked.

"I wait for him, too. Manuel gave me his other key." Serina moved away to the wide, sagging bed and sat down wearily on the edge of it. There was no place else to sit. The room was very small, with only the bed and the bureau.

"This is the safest place for me," she told him. "I don't want to show myself outside. Manuel thinks some of the Mexicans in the town are spies."

"For General Otero?" Clayburn suggested.

She looked up at him sharply, suddenly on her guard. "You know where Juan Ramirez has gone? And for what reason?"

"No. Do you?"

A curtain seemed to close behind Serina's eyes, and he knew he wasn't going to learn any more from her than he had from Manuel.

"Manuel was right," she said slowly, puzzled. "You are not one of us. . . . But then why are you here, waiting for Juan Ramirez?"

"He's my friend," Clayburn said simply.

But the truth went deeper than friendship.

Clayburn's father and the Ramirez family had had small neighboring ranches in northern New Mexico. His mother had died when he was two. He was twelve when his father was killed in a stampede. Diego and Adela Ramirez had taken him in, raising him with their own son, Juan. The two boys had become brothers in every way. This included constantly trying to beat the hell out of each other, when they weren't pitting themselves together against all the other kids in the nearest town. It also included a keen sense of rivalry in everything Diego Ramirez taught the two of them about handling cattle, horses—and guns. Clayburn had become the better marksman, but never managed to match the speed of Juan's draw. And in this and everything else, stocky, patient Diego Ramirez drew as much prideful pleasure from the steady sharpening of Clayburn's skills as he did from those of his real son.

In all, Clayburn had stayed with the Ramirez family for four years before the wanderlust that grew with his inches finally made him head off on his own.

It was after the death of Adela Ramirez that Diego had moved to Mexico with Juan to start a horse ranch. Clayburn had quit a job scouting Apaches for the army to join them and help out. He'd stayed for a year. Then the old restlessness had begun eating at him again. Diego and Juan had been doing fine when he'd left—what with plenty of wild mustangs south of the border and the army paying high prices for mounts north of the border. But since then, apparently, General Otero had come along. . . .

Clayburn looked at Serina sitting on the edge of his bed. "I don't suppose I can get you to tell me something about this Otero business."

Serina yawned. "I am very tired. I have been riding all day. And last night. Now I need some sleep."

And with that she tugged off her boots, loosened her belt, and stretched out on the lumpy mattress like a long slim cat.

Humor softened the hard lines on either side of Clayburn's mouth. "I may need some sleep too, later tonight."

She shrugged and linked her hands behind her head. "It's a wide bed."

Clayburn looked from her to the rest of the mattress and back to her. "Wide enough," he agreed softly.

Her dark eyes stared straight up at him. "Don't decide to do anything foolish when you do come to bed," she warned him softly. "I have very sharp nails."

Something warmed in the green depths of Clayburn's eyes. "I'd have bet on that." He was tempted to stay, and find out what a shared bottle of wine would make of her. But she did look weary. And there was that poker game waiting for him. Win or lose, she'd still be here, later. With some sleep in her.

Clayburn picked her knife off the floor and put it on the bureau. Then he took up his Winchester .44 carbine from the corner and started for the door.

Serina came up on one elbow, eyeing the carbine. "Where are you going?"

"To raise some cash."

She sat up straighter, her eyes widening.

Clayburn grinned. "Not that way. I'm going to sell it, not pull a stick-up. I'm in the middle of a poker game and I'm flat broke."

A thought came to him. "You have any money you could lend me? I'll pay it back with interest."

"No," she told him curtly. "When you are losing so bad you should stop while you still have something left."

"I've got a weak character," Clayburn told her amiably.

Serina looked at him scornfully. "I have known other men like you." She lay back on the bed and rolled over presenting her back to him, as though dismissing him from her thoughts. "You all die poor."

"Usually," Clayburn agreed, and went out.

He went down the steps and into the restaurant and braced Manuel. The restaurant owner reluctantly lent him all he could, thirty dollars. Clayburn left the adobe building and walked up the street to the livery stable. He sold his carbine and saddle, and the horse he'd bought the first day he'd arrived in Tubavi Springs. When he returned to the saloon he had two hundred and ten dollars in his pocket.

Hogan entered the gambling room in the back of the saloon five minutes later. In time to see Clayburn rake in a fair-sized pot, count it, and drop the required five dollars into the house cashbox.

Clayburn smiled at the scowling cattleman across the table from him as he gathered up the cards. "Poker luck is a shifty thing. Want to quit now, while you're still the big winner?"

"I broke you once," the cattleman growled. "I will again."

"Most likely," Clayburn conceded mildly, and began shuffling the cards with a smooth, flowing motion of his lean, rope-scarred hands.

Hogan pretended to be torn between the dice tables and blackjack. After a bit, he decided Clayburn would stay put awhile. Leaving the saloon, he started back down the street to spend some time around that Mexican restaurant. . . .

* * *

Juan Ramirez rode out of the night into the streets of Tubavi Springs on a tired horse, his shabby trail clothes covered with the dust of long riding. He was a solidly built, darkly handsome man with eyes older than they should have been; with savage bitterness masking what had once been an easy-going, good-natured face. Living for revenge did things to a man.

He studied both sides of the street with care as he approached the restaurant in the Mexican section of town. But he did not see the thin figure standing in the shadows of the alley next to it.

Reining to a halt in front of the restaurant, he swung down from his horse and was hitching the reins to the rail when Hogan's voice sounded behind him:

"Well, well . . . Juan Ramirez, himself."

Juan went for his gun as he spun toward the voice, seeing Hogan and the Colt in Hogan's hand pointing at his middle as his own hand closed around the butt of his holstered weapon.

He was very fast. But he had his gun only part way out of its holster when Hogan's finger tightened and the Colt in his hand roared.

The impact of the bullet drove Juan Ramirez back against his horse. The horse jumped and shied away from him. Juan tilted forward clutching his side and fell on his knees, the gun spilling from his fingers. He toppled over and rolled on his back, his lips stretching in a grimace of agony. A thin, unpleasant sound came through his clenched teeth.

Hogan looked down at him over the Colt, his face tight with anger. He hadn't expected the other man to try to draw against a gun already aimed point-blank at him. "*Damn* you, Ramirez, don't die on me. I want to deliver you to Dietrich alive."

THREE

Clayburn had four hundred and fifteen dollars in front of him when he was dealt a three of diamonds, a pair of jacks and a pair of aces. The white-haired cattleman, sitting on the dealer's left, opened for a stiff thirty dollars. The man on his left folded. The next man stayed for the thirty. Clayburn pushed thirty dollars in the pot, and the dealer folded. That left Clayburn, the cattleman and the other player in the game.

The cattleman discarded and drew two cards. The other man took one. Clayburn discarded the three of diamonds. The dealer slid him a card off the top of the deck. Clayburn picked it up. And had a third jack for a full house.

The cattleman's face was expressionless as he bet fifty dollars. The other man gave a disgusted grunt and quit, having failed to hit a straight.

A straight groove deepened across Clayburn's forehead. Otherwise his face showed nothing as he studied his pair of aces and three jacks. The cattleman's opening bet and two discards meant he'd started with three of a kind. His next bet of fifty meant he'd either gotten a pair for a full house or made it four of a kind. If it was a full house, he couldn't have three aces. At best, he'd drawn two aces, matching Clayburn's pair. If he had three kings or queens they'd beat Clayburn's three jacks. And he'd win with four of a kind. Any other combination would lose. The odds were in Clayburn's favor.

''Bump it fifty,'' Clayburn said, and counted one hundred dollars into the pot.

The cattleman's face didn't change, but he hesitated—which ruled out the possibility of his having four of a kind. "Raise you another fifty," he said after a moment, and put a hundred in the pot.

It was Clayburn's three jacks against whatever three of a kind the cattleman held. Only queens or kings could beat the jacks—as against any one of nine other possibilities that would lose to them.

"Let's make it a hundred more," Clayburn drawled lazily, and put a hundred and fifty in the pot.

The cattleman's mouth thinned. He studied Clayburn's eyes, but saw nothing there except his own reflection. He studied his own hand again. The seconds dragged by.

"The game," Clayburn reminded him quietly, "is poker. See the raise or fold."

The cattleman flushed. "See it," he rasped, and slowly counted another hundred dollars into the pot.

When the last of the cattleman's money was in, Clayburn spread his hand out face up.

The cattleman cursed viciously and threw his own hand down—two aces and three nines.

Clayburn dropped five dollars in the house cashbox and raked in his winnings. He now had seven hundred and twenty dollars. And was beginning to think of Serina waiting in his room over the Mexican restaurant.

The cattleman gathered up what money he had left and shoved to his feet. "I should've quit while I was ahead. I'm quitting now."

Clayburn looked up at him—and saw Serina come in through the door from the bar.

Her eyes searched the crowded gambling room till they met Clayburn's. One look at her face, and he gave a sharp nod. She turned and hurried out.

Clayburn stood and stuffed the money in his pockets. "Time for me to quit, too." Ignoring the startled looks on the faces of the other players, he put on his hat and went out. Serina wasn't in the saloon. He found her in the night shadows outside, standing stiffly against the wall.

"What happened?"

"Juan Ramirez came back," she told him tensely, almost whispering. "A man named Hogan was waiting for him, and shot him when. . . ."

"How bad is he hurt?" Clayburn demanded quietly, his face wooden.

"I don't know. Bad, I think. I am afraid to go to him. He is in the jail."

Clayburn's forehead creased. "Why?"

Serina shook her head helplessly. "I don't know. The marshal came after the shooting. He talked to Hogan. Then they carried Ramirez to the jail. Manuel says they sent for a doctor. . . ."

Clayburn rubbed the knuckles of his left hand along the line of his jaw. His eyes were narrow and thoughtful. "Who is this Hogan?"

"A man who hunts other men. A man who kills. For pay. Otero pays him."

"Uh-huh," Clayburn said, without meaning. He drummed his fingertips against his thigh, squinting off up the street. Then he touched Serina's shoulder. "Go wait for me in my room."

She looked at him gravely. "What are you going to do?"

"I don't know yet," he told her, and started off up the street with long steps that covered distance swiftly without any appearance of hurrying.

The jail and law office were in a long, one-storey adobe-brick building. It had only one door, opening into the marshal's office in the front part of the building. Clayburn knew two of the three men who were in the lamp-lit office when he stepped inside out of the night. Marshal Benedict sat behind his desk with his plump thumbs hooked in the armholes of his vest, puffing on a cigar. He was a stout, florid man with a bland expression and greedy eyes. Benedict was more than the law in Tubavi Springs. He also owned the saloon and its gambling room, the hotel, and the general store. Wearing a badge helped him to keep anyone from opening competition for any one of those.

One of the marshal's deputies leaned against the wall beside the door leading back to the two jail cells. His name was

Harris, and Clayburn had never seen him without that sawed-
off shotgun in the crook of his arm.

The third man in the office, a very thin man with a sharp
face, rested a hip on the corner of the marshal's desk and
looked Clayburn over with pale, expressionless eyes.

"You've got a friend of mine here," Clayburn told Marshal Benedict. "Juan Ramirez. I understand he's hurt."

The marshall nodded pleasantly. "Doc Hall's back in his
cell with him now, gettin' the slug out. Friend of yours, is
he?"

"Why do you have him here?" Clayburn asked, his tone
flat and unemotional.

Marshal Benedict took the cigar from between his yellow
teeth and looked at it with distaste. "He's wanted in Mexico.
For murder."

"Who says?"

The skinny man lounging on the corner of the desk said,
"Me."

Clayburn looked at him. "Your name Hogan?"

"That's right."

Clayburn studied him. Then he looked again at the marshal. "You taking his word for it?"

"Nope. Mr. Hogan gave me a warrant for Ramirez. Signed
by General Otero himself. Wanna see it?"

Clayburn shook his head. He was quite certain Hogan had
given the marshal more than a warrant. Benedict was a man
who'd take a bribe without blinking. "That warrant's no good
here in United States territory."

The marshal dropped his cigar on the floor and ground it
out with his heel. "Maybe so. But Tubavi Springs is awful
close to Mexico. I like to keep good relations."

"Marshal!" a voice called from back in the cells.

Benedict nodded at his deputy. "Go let the doc out."

Deputy Harris took down a ring of keys from a wall peg
and went through the inside door carrying them in one hand
and his shotgun in the other. Moments later he came back,
followed by Dr. Hall.

"How is he?" Clayburn asked quietly.

The doctor shifted his black satchel to his left hand and

scratched his beard with his right thumbnail. "I got the bullet out and took care of the wound. It was close, but he's got a sound constitution. He'll recover, with enough rest and tending."

Hogan spoke up. "How long before he can ride?"

The doctor shrugged a shoulder. "A week. At least. If you want him to live." He scowled at the marshal. "I take it I won't get paid for this."

Marshal Benedict smiled innocently. "Your civic duty, Doc."

The doctor grunted angrily and stomped out of the building.

Hogan turned to the marshal. "A week. That's more'n enough time for the other men I sent for to get here and help me take Ramirez back."

Clayburn looked at Hogan. "You need help?" His tone was deliberately insolent.

Hogan stared back at him, the corners of his thin mouth turning down. "There's a bunch of outlaw rebels still loose in Sonora. Ramirez is one of their leaders. I'm making sure I get him where I'm taking him. And just what's your interest in it?"

"I told you. We're friends."

"Maybe it's more than that," Hogan suggested slowly. "Maybe I ought to take you along, too."

Clayburn got an almost sleepy look. "I don't think so."

Marshal Benedict shook his head. "Me neither, Hogan. He's an American citizen."

"So is Ramirez," Clayburn said, his voice brittle. "He was born in Santa Fe. I can get proof of that, easy enough."

"That don't matter," the marshal replied indifferently. "He's still a Mex, wherever he was born. Mexico's where he's wanted and Mexico's where he belongs."

Clayburn's gaze slipped from Hogan to Deputy Harris to the marshal. There was no point in arguing. When it came to bribing, he couldn't match what General Otero could offer Marshal Benedict. Going against the three of them would be suicide. Hogan alone was formidable enough. And Marshal Benedict didn't control a town like this with just talk. As for the deputy, he didn't carry that shotgun because it was ornamental. And there were two day deputies who also carried shotguns when they were on duty.

"I want to see Ramirez," Clayburn told the marshal.

Benedict waved an indulgent hand. "Sure. Go ahead. Just don't spend too long at it."

Clayburn crossed the office and stepped through the inside doorway. The two jail cells were side by side, small windowless cubicles with iron-bar doors locked shut. One of them was empty. In the other Juan Ramirez lay on a flat straw pallet on the floor, unconscious. He was stripped to the waist. Heavy bandaging was wrapped around the lower part of his broad chest. Clayburn observed the way he was breathing and the slack, drained look of his face.

When Clayburn turned away from the bars he found Hogan standing in the doorway, watching him. Clayburn started towards him, hands dangling at his sides. Hogan stepped aside to let him enter the office.

Marshal Benedict was tilted back in his chair with one leg up on the desk. "Look like he'll live?"

"He'll live," Clayburn said shortly.

"Too bad he's a friend of yours. But there ain't anything you can do about it. You might's well get back to your gambling."

Something flickered in Clayburn's eyes. Then it was gone, leaving no change in his expression. "I just might do that."

The marshal smiled his friendly smile. "Sure. And why'nt you try my craps tables for a change? Make money faster that way than with poker."

"Lose it faster, too." Clayburn's lips formed a smile that was as friendly as Benedict's. And as genuine.

"Well, one thing you can be sure of in my town. The games ain't rigged. You know that."

Clayburn knew it. Cheating the kind of men who drifted through Tubavi Springs, would be too risky—even for a man as greedy and deadly as Benedict. He glanced sideways at Hogan, his smile harmless, his eyes opaque. Then he nodded at the marshal and strolled out of the office.

When he was outside in the darkness, he moved faster.

FOUR

Serina was sitting tensely on the edge of his bed. She jumped to her feet as he came in. "Well?"

He shut the door and told her what he had learned in the jail. His voice was slow and deliberate, his eyes narrow and thoughtful. "Once those men Hogan sent to Sonora for show up it'll be too late to do anything."

"What can we do?" It was a question, not a protest.

He told her. He didn't insult her by warning her of the danger she'd put herself in if she took part in it. She wasn't the kind that talk frightened. And he didn't want to try. He'd need her to get it done.

As he talked, he opened his saddlebags and took out a pair of dice. Then, from inside his left sleeve, he drew out a flat-handled, narrow-bladed knife from the soft buckskin sheath strapped to the inside of his forearm. He sat on the edge of the bed and began shaving the edges of the dice carefully with the blade of the knife.

Serina watched, her eyes bright with interest, hearing him out. When he finished talking she got a worried look. "But the doctor said he must rest for a week. If he's moved so soon, he might die."

"Maybe," Clayburn agreed. "But if he's not moved he'll die and no maybe about it."

He rattled the dice in his fist and cast them on the floor, watching the way they rolled and came to a stop. He did it again. Then twice more.

He picked up one of them, shaved two of its edges a bit

more, and tossed it on the floor. When it came to a stop, he picked it up and tossed it again. Again.

Satisfied, he slid the knife back into its concealment inside his left sleeve, stood up and stuffed the dice down in his pocket with the money he'd won at poker. "That horse Ramirez rode in on still in front?"

She nodded.

He didn't have to ask if she'd help. Her face told that plainly enough. There was a firm set to her mouth and an almost wild eagerness in her eyes that made her even more exciting to be near.

"Where's your horse?" he asked her.

"The stable."

He picked up his saddlebags and gave them to her, told her what to do as they went down the steps together. Leaving the building alone, he went to the livery stable, bought back his horse, saddle and carbine, got Serina's horse, and saddled both of them. Sliding the carbine into his saddle scabbard, he led the horses through back alleys to the rear of the Mexican restaurant.

Serina was waiting there with Ramirez's horse. "Manuel is getting the food for us," she said. "And clean cloths for bandages."

"Make sure all the canteens are full," he told her, and left her with the three horses.

The saloon was doing its peak business of the night when Clayburn entered. He pushed through the noisy crowd to the gambling room. There were more men in it than when he'd left. Mule skinners, cowhands, miners, drifters, renegades— rough men, with a lot of short-fused violence locked inside them.

Clayburn turned his back on the three poker tables. He strolled past the men crowding the monte, hazard and faro games. With an appearance of aimless indecision he approached one of the two craps tables. For a time he just stood there watching the play. On one side a bunch of young Texas trail hands were losing heavily and not liking it. The house gambler chanted encouragement to them in a sing-song voice as he raked in their money and rolled the dice back to them.

Clayburn's eyes slid to the bouncer seated on a high stool on the other side of the room, a gun on each hip and a lead-weighted club conspicuous across his knees. There was another like him out in the saloon. And a house shotgun under the bar.

Elbowing his way closer to the craps table, Clayburn got some money from his pocket—not the one containing the dice he'd shaved. He began making small side-bets, winning a little, losing less.

One of the Texans got the dice, placed his bet, waited till his friends put their money on him, and rolled. The dice came up with a six and a two. The Texan grinned confidently. Clayburn bet five dollars he wouldn't make the point.

"Eight's the point," the house gambler chanted. "Eight any old way at all. . . ."

The Texan drew five. Then ten. And then threw craps. The Texans glared as the house man raked in their losings and forked over Clayburn's winnings.

The man on Clayburn's left got the dice; a hulking mule skinner with a battered face. He threw a seven. Then another. Then an eleven. Clayburn bet against him each time, lost each time, doubled his bet each time. The mule skinner, his winnings piled up in front of him, turned an exultant face Clayburn's way.

"You're makin' a mistake, friend. Bet with me. I'm hot."

Clayburn smiled. "Hot goes cold sooner or later."

The hulking mule skinner shook his head. "I'll feel it before it happens." He bet all the money in front of him, shook the dice lovingly in his huge fist, and cast them.

They rolled across the table and came to a stop showing four and two.

"Six is the point. . . ." the house man chanted.

Happily, the mule skinner picked up the dice, rattled them and tossed.

He didn't make it. His grin drained away as he watched all that money being raked in by the house.

Clayburn picked up the dice, bet fifteen dollars. He threw a seven the first time out. He let his winnings stand, and added the rest of the money in his hand. This time he threw ten—and made his point after five more rolls. Grinning, he bet all his winnings on himself, dug into his right-hand pocket for more money.

His hand came out of the pocket dangling fifty dollars between thumb and forefinger. The shaved dice were concealed in the palm of his hand, held in the crease against its heel.

He dropped the fifty on the pile of winnings. "Bet it all!" He picked up the house dice with his left hand, appeared to switch them to his right.

But the dice he rattled in his right fist were his own. He threw them hard. As they jumped across the table toward the house man, taking all eyes with them, Clayburn let the house dice slide from his left hand into his pants pocket.

The dice came to rest. "Craps . . ." the house gambler sang out. "Too bad."

Clayburn got a shocked look as the house man raked in all his money and forked the dice over to the next man—a tall, leathery freighter.

The freighter took up the dice, plunked down his money, and threw.

"Craps again. . . ." the house man chanted sadly. He raked in the money, reached for the dice.

Clayburn slapped his stick away. "Wait a minute!" he said, very suddenly and very loudly. "I want a look at those damn dice of yours!"

There was an abrupt quietening in the room. He had the attention of everyone in the place. Other men began drifting over to the table as Clayburn picked up the dice. The bouncer got down off his high stool, the club dangling in his left hand.

Around the table, everyone was watching Clayburn as he studied the dice, turning them between his thumb and forefinger. First one, then the other.

"That's what I thought," he announced finally. "They're ringers! No wonder we all lose as soon as we start winning big. They ring phony dice into the game every time."

A low ominous growling sound began to spread around the gambling room. Everyone was on his feet now.

Clayburn turned to the mule skinner. "Look."

The mule skinner took the dice, stared at them blankly. "I don't know. . . ."

"Roll 'em."

The mule skinner tossed the dice on the table. They came up craps. He rolled again. The same thing happened. "By God, they *are* phonies!"

"Damn right!" Clayburn shouted indignantly. "Every game in this place must be rigged. They've been cheating all of us . . . robbing us blind!"

The house man began backing nervously away from the table. The bouncer appeared, eyeing Clayburn menacingly, hefting his lead-weighted club. "Hold on a . . ."

The hulking mule skinner slammed his fist against the back of the bouncer's neck. The bouncer went down as if he'd been hit with an anvil.

"Let's take our money back!" somebody yelled. Men began snatching at the cash on the tables and somebody else hollered threateningly: "Hey! That's *mine*!"

There was the sound of knuckles connecting with a jaw. Clayburn seized the edge of the dice table and overturned it, scattering all the money on the floor. Men began knocking each other aside, falling on their knees to grab fistfuls of cash. Clayburn picked up a chair and hurled it full-force at the rear window.

The smash of shattering glass triggered the explosion. The next second all hell broke loose in the gambling room: tables overturning, chairs being smashed against the walls, men fighting over fallen money, the house gamblers battling to form a defensive knot in one corner; yelling, groaning, splintering wood. . . .

The saloon bouncer appeared in the doorway, clubbed a trail hand to the floor, and went down under an avalanche of enraged Texans and mule skinners. The violence poured out into the saloon. Somebody roared, "Tear the place apart!" There was an eruption of savage shouting, gunshots, breaking bottles.

Clayburn fought his way out of a struggling tangle of men gone wild, and backed away toward the rear door.

* * *

It was one of the day deputies that came running into Marshal Benedict's office with the news of what was happening on the other side of town.

"They're breaking your saloon wide open, Marshal! Taking all the money in the place! Smashing your . . ."

The marshal was already on his feet, charging out of the jailhouse as fast as he could go. Deputy Harris and the day deputy rushed out after him, pounding off up the street in his wake.

That left only Hogan in the marshal's office. He stood up slowly, a faint feeling of edginess annoying him. His pale eyes went to the door leading to the cells, shifted to the door leading in from the street. After a moment, he pulled a straight-backed chair over into a corner of the office and sat down again with his back protected by the wall juncture, watching the front door and window. His thin right hand moved and came to rest on the grip of his gun.

He was reaching into his pocket for a cigar when Serina came in off the street. She was wearing a wide-brimmed hat and her Levi's were stuffed down inside riding boots. Without looking at Hogan she moved straight toward the door to the cells, the tightness of her mouth the only sign of nervousness in an otherwise expressionless face.

Hogan came up off his chair with his voice cracking like a whip: "Stop right there!"

Serina paused and gave him a passing glance, an almost stupid blankness in her dark eyes. Then she continued toward the inner door.

Hogan caught her arm, jerking her to a halt and swinging her around to face him. Her response was startling in its swiftness. Hogan winced as four sharp nails drew fiery scratches across his cheek.

He cursed viciously and slapped her across the face, hard. Serina was knocked against the wall; bounced away from it with the fingers of both hands clawing for his eyes. Hogan struck her again, this time with the full force of his bony fist. She fell against the wall and hung there sagging, dazed, the reddened side of her face beginning to swell.

Clayburn stepped into the office behind Hogan holding his

Colt in one hand. "I'm aiming at the small of your back," he said quietly and distinctly. "At this range I can't miss."

Hogan froze in position, his pale eyes going empty. He did not turn his head or move in any other way.

"Unbuckle your gunbelt," Clayburn told him evenly. "I'm not going to start counting. Do it or I break your spine with my first bullet. Do it *now*."

Hogan's hands obeyed the command automatically. He wasn't fool enough to make a play when he hadn't a chance, and what was in Clayburn's voice told him he had none now. The gunbelt thudded to the floor with its holstered gun.

"Back up," Clayburn ordered.

Hogan took two backward steps.

"Keep coming."

Hogan backed up another step. Another . . .

The barrel of Clayburn's gun whipped against the side of his head, just above the ear. Hogan went down in a heap and stayed the way he fell.

Clayburn holstered the Colt and stepped over Hogan's unconscious form. "Serina!" His voice was harsh.

She pushed herself away from the wall, swaying a little, blinking her dazed eyes. Her hand came up slowly to touch her bruised face.

"Are you all right?" he asked, with more impatience than concern. He needed her functioning, not out on her feet.

A sneer masked her pain. "It is not the first time a man has hit me. Men like to hit women. It makes them feel brave."

Clayburn took the ring of keys down from the peg and went through to the cells. Juan Ramirez still lay unconscious on his straw pallet. Unlocking the iron-bar door, Clayburn entered the cell and went down on one knee beside the pallet.

"Juan!"

There was no response.

"Juan!" Clayburn's thumb and forefinger closed on the wounded Mexican's cheek, pinched cruelly. Juan Ramirez made a small sound in his throat and moved his head slightly, but did not come to.

Clayburn's mouth twitched in a grimace of irritation. He

got both arms under Ramirez and lifted him with an effort, grunting softly as he rose to his feet. He carried his limp, heavy body out to the office.

Serina was standing by the door to the street, Hogan's gun in her hand. As Clayburn appeared, she stepped outside and looked around quickly, hearing the faint, distant sounds of the riot on the other side of town. She motioned with one hand. Clayburn followed her out of the building.

They turned into the first alley they came to, staying in its narrow darkness till they reached the eastern edge of town. Manuel was there, holding the three saddled horses. As soon as they arrived he left without a word, hurrying back to his restaurant.

Clayburn raised Juan up onto his own buckskin horse, with Serina's help. She turned out to have more strength to her than he would have guessed. They got Juan straddling the horse, in the saddle. Clayburn put a toe in the stirrup and swung up behind Juan Ramirez, his right arm around his limp form to hold him in the saddle, his left hand taking the reins. Serina mounted her own horse and got hold of the lead rope secured to the horse Ramirez had ridden into town. They started east away from Tubavi Springs, riding into the night toward the Chiricahua Mountains.

They rode slowly. But they had gone only a mile when Clayburn's right hand became wet with the blood soaking through Juan's bandages.

FIVE

Hogan rode out of Tubavi Springs with the first light of dawn, together with two of Marshal Benedict's deputies, following the tracks of the horses on which Clayburn, Serina and Juan Ramirez had escaped.

He wasn't too worried about the five-hour lead the fugitives had, knowing they couldn't ride too fast with Juan Ramirez wounded that badly. Not without killing him.

Two miles outside the town the tracks vanished across an area of rock rubble stretching along the base of a long mesa. Hogan and the two deputies spread out, circling until one of them spotted where the tracks showed again in the dirt surface beyond the rock rubble. Then the three of them rode on, pushing their mounts fast along the trail that led south toward the border.

Up in a shadowed pocket of the mesa wall's rock formations, Clayburn watched them go—following Serina and the three horses. She would leave a nice clear trail for them, until she was well south of the border.

When the pursuers disappeared over the horizon Clayburn lowered his carbine and turned back into the pocket in the rock formations. Juan lay there in the shade, still unconscious but breathing easier and no longer bleeding through the new bandaging covering his wound. Clayburn settled down beside him to wait.

It was late afternoon when the two deputies reappeared from the south, heading for Tubavi Springs. As had been anticipated by Clayburn, they'd turned back at the border.

Hogan wasn't with them, having apparently pushed on into Mexico. Clayburn wasn't worried about him catching Serina. She was too far ahead of him by now; and she could keep going at a fast, steady clip with those three horses to ride. And she'd told him she knew of a section of cross-cut stone canyons she could reach by nightfall, where the horses would leave no tracks by which Hogan could follow her any further.

Clayburn had had to do some determined persuading to talk Serina out of the notion of killing Hogan before they went into that jail. Killing Hogan would have meant Marshal Benedict could have pinned a murder charge on Clayburn. This way, Benedict was unlikely to make any charges against him to the law outside Tubavi Springs. He couldn't charge Clayburn with breaking a man out of his jail without getting into an embarrassing explanation of why Juan had been in his jail in the first place.

Shortly after the deputies rode back, Juan Ramirez regained consciousness. Enough to drink some water. Enough for his eyes to focus on Clayburn and recognize him. Not enough for him to show any surprise.

Clayburn sat on the ground beside Juan, feeding him more water a little at a time and bringing him up to date on what had happened. Including Serina's message:

"She said she came up here to warn you that Gustavo's place is no longer safe for you to return to. They'll be waiting for you in Arizeda instead. You understand what I'm saying?"

Juan nodded faintly and tried to speak. But it was too difficult for him, and he finally closed his eyes instead and went back to sleep. A real sleep this time.

His fever subsided as he slept. When he awoke again at dusk his eyes were clearer. He was still very weak, but he was able to drink more, eat a little—and talk.

"You finally came," he said. His voice was a dragging whisper, drained of any emotion.

"As soon as I got the message," Clayburn told him. "It took a long time to catch up with me."

"That's all right now . . . I've taken care of it . . . myself."

A furrow deepened between Clayburn's eyes. "Taken care of what?"

"Guns. We need them down there. . . . Winchester repeaters. . . . That's what I wanted you to do for us up here . . . arrange for us to buy them . . . a lot of them. But I didn't hear from you . . . so I came north and handled it myself."

"I don't know exactly what's going on down there," Clayburn said slowly, "but it sounds like you've got yourself mixed up in a Mexican mess that's none of your business. Every time they have one of these little revolutions, the ones that take over turn out to be as bad as the ones they took over from. So it doesn't matter *who* wins. I don't know how you got tangled up in it, but my advice'd be to get out. Now. The same goes for Diego—if he's mixing in too."

Juan stared up at him for a time in silence. "Then you don't know?"

Clayburn felt something very cold in the pit of his stomach. "Tell me."

"My father is dead. He was hung . . . by a man named Dietrich."

By dawn of the next morning Clayburn had the whole story. Diego Ramirez and his son had pretty much ignored the various factions fighting for political and military control of their section of Sonora. And since the Ramirez ranch had grown enormously over the years, and acquired a tough crew of vaqueros, the various factions had in turn left them alone. Until Otero had taken over.

It was believed that Otero had acquired the backing of some international mining interests. At any rate, he'd gotten from somewhere enough money to hire Dietrich and his mercenaries. Dietrich was a soldier of fortune who'd previously fought in South America, China, the Middle East—wherever there was rebellion, revolution, civil war. The men he led—some thirty-five of them—were of all kinds, alike in only one thing: each was an experienced fighting man, a trained killer.

After Dietrich and his killers had eliminated the leadership of the opposing factions, Otero had been able to assume command of all the surviving Sonoran troops. Then Dietrich's bunch and Otero's army had combined to begin wiping out everyone who tried to resist Otero's rule, seize

possession of all the arms and ammunition within Otero's
domain, and impose a heavy, ruinous taxation on everything
the people owned, grew or raised.

But they'd been smart enough to strike first at the biggest
groups that might possibly give them trouble in the future—
striking before anyone knew what they had in mind. And one
of the first places they'd struck had been the Ramirez ranch.

Juan was far away in the Sierra Madre mountains at the
time, hunting wild horses with half the crew. Dietrich and
his gang had showed up at the ranch, demanding that Diego
turn over half of the Ramirez horses and cattle, plus all weapons. Diego had refused. The battle that he'd been able to put
up with his greatly outnumbered crew had been stubborn,
violent, and short—ending the only way it could. And Diego,
wounded, had been taken prisoner.

The other wounded prisoners were killed on the spot. But
Diego had been taken alive to the nearest large town. And
there, before all the forceably assembled townspeople, Dietrich had hanged him. As an example and a warning.

Then Dietrich had set up a trap to wipe out Juan with the
rest of the Ramirez crew when they returned from the mountains. But they'd been warned in time, and had slipped back
into the Sierra Madre. Juan had gone into hiding with a few of
the crew who'd been with the Ramirez ranch long enough to
regard the hanging of old Diego as a personal matter. Soon
other men had begun slipping into the mountains to join Juan.
Men motivated by the same hatred and lust for revenge because
of Dietrich's forays against their ranches, haciendas or towns.

"What about this Serina?" Clayburn asked Juan. "Where
does she fit in all this?"

"Her brother's in this with me. Sort of my second-in-
command." There was a slight pause. "His name's Latigo.
Rafael Latigo." Juan said it without emphasis; the name
spoke for itself.

Clayburn's right eyebrow quirked up, just a fraction.

Juan nodded wearily. "That's right . . . Latigo. Wanted on
both sides of the border. An outlaw, a killer—and you know
what, Clay? That doesn't matter a bit to the rest of us. He's
what we need. Him and a couple others he brought in with him.

They know how to fight and they're used to playing hide-and-seek with the law. All that matters to us is, they're on our side.''

"But not for the same reasons," Clayburn said softly.

"We know that. And for the time being, we don't care." Juan raised a shaky hand, forced it into a fist and looked at it dully, then let it drop. "Right now we'll take any kind of help we can get."

The trouble was, Juan's group was far too small to go up against Dietrich's gang and Otero's army. There were hundreds of men eager to join Juan. The people of the country hated Otero. But these others had nothing to fight with. The few weapons some had managed to hide were mostly ancient muzzle-loaders. Nothing that could stand up against cannons and six-shooters, twelve-shot carbines and fifteen-shot repeating rifles in the hands of trained professionals.

That was what Juan had wanted Clayburn to handle for them: the purchase and delivery of a shipment of enough modern guns and ammunition to arm a force big enough to have some chance against Otero and Dietrich. But now that Juan had taken care of this himself, there was another problem. And towards evening of the second day, when Juan was strong enough to sit up with his back braced against a rock and feed himself, he told Clayburn about it:

"The people I contacted have agreed to supply us with all the Model '73 Winchesters we need to arm the people, and enough ammunition for them. For a price. Thirty thousand dollars."

Clayburn whistled softly.

Juan nodded. "It's a stiff price, Clay. But we're not in a position to bargain. The people I talked to knew that, of course."

"Do you *have* that much money?"

"Some of it. Not all." Juan looked directly at Clayburn. "I'm well enough to take care of myself now, with this food and water we've got here. But I'm not strong enough to ride. And right now every day counts. It's gonna take time for Latigo to get hold of the rest of that price."

He let it go at that, waiting.

Clayburn said, as Juan had known he would, "I'll get the message to him."

They looked at each other in silence for a time, two men with a lot of shared memories between them. Both thinking of a dead man who'd once shared those same memories with them. . . .

When night came, Clayburn slipped back into Tubavi Springs and gave Manuel money to buy two good horses for him. In the darkness, he managed to get out of the town without being spotted, taking the two horses back to the place where he'd left Juan.

Juan was still awake, leaning against the dark rock, waiting for him.

"Tell Latigo I'll come as soon as I can make it," he said to Clayburn as they parted. "He can leave word in Oputo, to let me know where to find him by then."

Clayburn nodded. "I'll tell him."

Juan hesitated. "Maybe I'll see you, if you're still down there when I. . . ."

"I'll still be there," Clayburn told him quietly.

He left one horse with Juan. On the other, a strapping sorrel, he rode south through the shadows toward Sonora; to deliver Juan's message to Latigo. But that was only a small part of the reason.

Most of the reason was a man named Dietrich.

The man who had hanged Diego Ramirez.

Clayburn didn't give a damn who wound up running any part of Sonora. But one thing he was quite sure of:

He would not return from Sonora until Dietrich was dead.

The walled ruins of Arizeda huddled in the bottom of a semi-arid gorge in the Western Sierra Madre, an empty ghost town baking in the remorseless golden heat of the late morning sun. A once-prosperous silver mining town founded way back in the early seventeen hundreds, it had been abandoned over half a century ago when the rich ore in the mountain behind it had played out. This was where Serina had said Latigo and the others were waiting for Juan.

Clayburn looked down at Arizeda from the shadow of a mottled sandstone butte. There was no sign of life among the ruins below him. No horses, no men, no smoke. Clayburn frowned and shifted a little in the saddle to ease leg and back muscles sore from hours of steady riding over rough country.

There was nothing of the gambler about his appearance now. In place of his city clothes he wore his battered slouch hat and old trail boots, a hard-used buckskin shirt and faded Levi's. They were the clothes of a man who'd long been part of an open, hazardous land, enduring its long droughts and sudden cloudbursts and driving dust storms. A special breed of man who'd encountered and survived everything that could come at him from this land and its savage prowlers.

His eyes, slitted against the glare of the scorching sunlight, scanned the rest of the dry gorge, then shifted back to the town. Finally, he drew his carbine from the saddle boot. Holding it ready, he kneed the sorrel horse away from the butte and down the sandy slope.

Skirting a tangle of rocks at the base of the slope, he followed an ancient ore-wagon road through a maze of boulders and stone pinnacles. Warily, he searched the shadows between the boulders, the shimmering heat haze rising off the slopes, the broken formations of a long, low cliff flanking the town ahead. Nothing moved in the silence around him.

There were gaping holes in many parts of the thick walls that had once protected Arizeda from Indian raids. Clayburn angled off the road toward one of these openings, avoiding the wide gateway. He rode through the wall into a wide street, pausing for a careful look around him. Cactus bushes were everywhere, growing up out of the worn cobbles of the street and the adobe brick walls of long-empty mansions. A wild fig tree filled the shadowed arch of an arcade to his left, its gnarled roots wrapped around two of the slender pillars. Bright-blossomed vines climbed the wrought-iron grillwork in doorways and dark windows. Ahead, in the center of the town, the bell tower of a church rose above the other roofs, ocotillo and prickly pear sprouting from its crumbling dun-colored bricks.

A feeling of danger crawled up Clayburn's spine as he rode deeper into the emptiness of the ancient town. Serina had come all the way to Tubavi Springs to tell Juan that this would be the safe place for him to return to. And it was only natural that the rebels would keep out of sight until they got a close look at him and saw who he was. But Clayburn's keyed-up senses kept warning him that something was not right here in Arizeda. His finger was tensed across the trigger of his carbine as he turned into a walled street leading toward the central plaza.

A man appeared out of an arched patio doorway in front of Clayburn, Clayburn reined to a halt with his left hand, bringing his carbine up to point at the man's chest.

The man smiled up at him with his mouth. He was a huge, hulking Mexican with a brutal face that did not become more pleasant because of the smile. He wore a gun strapped to his right hip, but his hands were empty.

"Whom do you seek?" he asked in Spanish.

"I don't understand Spanish," Clayburn lied, using the time to observe every doorway and window he could see without taking his eyes off the big Mexican.

"Who do you look for here?" the Mexican asked him in slow English.

"Nobody. Just riding through." The sense of danger was stronger, almost solid now.

The big Mexican's smile broadened. Behind Clayburn a Texas voice drawled: "Let go of the rifle, Mister. And get down."

Clayburn turned his head. A lean, hard-faced man stood there in the shade of an arcade-covered walk, pointing a Colt at the middle of his back. As Clayburn looked at him, three more men emerged from a dark doorway behind the Texan. None of them Mexican. Each holding an aimed gun on him.

Clayburn forced his fingers open and let the carbine fall to the thick dust covering the cobbled street. All of him was rigid as he swung down from the sorrel.

The hulking Mexican was still smiling at him. He pointed a thick finger. "The gunbelt."

The other four men were fanning out around him. The Texan on his right. A squat, bearded man on his left. The other two behind him.

"You heard him," the Texan drawled, moving the gun in

his hand a couple of inches for emphasis. "Take off that gunbelt."

Clayburn got a puzzled look on his face as his stiff fingers unbuckled the cartridge belt, let it drop with its holstered gun to the dust. "What is this? A holdup? I don't have anything anybody'd . . ."

"You're in trouble," the Texan cut in. "Bad trouble. You picked the wrong side."

"I don't know what you're talking about. Like I said, I'm just riding through and . . ."

The big Mexican drove a massive fist to the side of Clayburn's head. Clayburn rolled with the punch, but got enough of its bludgeoning force to twist him around and send him sprawling to the ground. He landed on his hands and knees, his brain spinning.

"That's just for openers," the Texan said above him. "What's your connection with Ramirez?"

Clayburn raised his head and looked up, his face wooden. "I don't know what you're talking about."

"Play games with us," the Texan warned him thinly, "and you'll hurt like you've never hurt in your life. You'll be a long time dying. . . . Nobody comes here any more unless they got a special reason. Like expectin' to find Ramirez."

Clayburn shoved to his feet, swaying. "You've got the wrong man."

The Mexican loomed closer. "Give him to me. He will talk."

The Texan considered Clayburn, then nodded. "Okay. He's all yours."

The Mexican's eyes dwelled on Clayburn's face, cruel with anticipation. "My name is Morales," he said softly. "You know of me?"

"No."

"But you know Juan Ramirez."

"No."

"I think you lie." Moralez began drawing a pair of blood-stained leather gloves on his massive, powerful hands. "Hold his arms," he told the two men behind Clayburn.

SIX

"Wait," Clayburn grated quickly, keeping his arms down tightly at his sides. "I'll talk."

Morales looked disappointed.

The Texan eyed Clayburn suspiciously. "You crack pretty damn easy. I didn't figure you to be that soft."

Clayburn shrugged. "Why get myself hurt for something I don't have any interest in. I don't owe them anything. They haven't paid me a red cent yet."

"Who hasn't? Ramirez?"

Clayburn gave the Texan a calculating look. "You said before I picked the wrong side. There still time for me to switch sides?"

"Maybe," the Texan said cautiously. "We can talk about that after we hear what you got to say."

Clayburn appeared to hesitate. "I ran into a man named Juan Ramirez up north. In Bisbee. Said he was hiring gunfighters for a little war down here. Two hundred a month and any loot I could pick up on the side. Been awhile since I had a job paid that much, so I figured what the hell. . . . Anyway, he sent me down here. Said I'd find some of his men here and . . ."

Clayburn got a puzzled look. "How come they're *not* here?"

"They were," the Texan told him. "We got a tip and a bunch of us came to take 'em. But they slipped away from us in the dark. Most of our men went after them. We stayed here, just in case any strays came along looking for them."

"And I'm what came along," Clayburn said disgustedly. "Well, do I get the chance to switch sides?"

"Depends. . . . Tell us the rest of it."

"That's all there is," Clayburn's voice was very sincere. "Juan Ramirez just sent me down to join up. Said he'd get here himself sometime tomorrow."

The squat, bearded men on the other side of Clayburn looked sharply at the Texan. "Say . . . wouldn't Dietrich like that just fine. If we show up with Juan Ramirez in tow."

The Texan nodded, but his eyes were still suspicious as they studied Clayburn. "You sure about that? He's coming here? If you're lying : . ."

"I'm not lying."

"Easy enough to find out," the squat, bearded man said. "All we got to do is wait. Then if Juan Ramirez don't show up, we can make this guy wish he was never born."

The Texan hadn't taken his eyes off Clayburn. "You heard what he just said?"

Clayburn nodded. "I heard."

"You still say Juan Ramirez is coming here tomorrow?"

"That's what he told me."

The Texan studied him for a moment longer. Then he went to the sorrel horse and cut a length of rope from the lariat looped on the saddle. "Put your hands behind your back," he said as he returned to Clayburn.

The squat, bearded man had his gun trained on Clayburn's stomach. There were two more guns aimed point-blank at his back. Clayburn put his arms behind him, the back of his right wrist across the inside of his left; to keep the Texan's fingers from touching the slim knife strapped inside his left sleeve. The rope was tied around his wrists, binding them together behind him. The hilt of the hidden knife bit into his wrist bones as the knots were tightened viciously.

Then the Texan stepped away, looking Clayburn in the face again. "We'll wait," he said slowly. "You know what's going to happen to you if Juan Ramirez doesn't show."

"I know," Clayburn said tonelessly.

The Texan glanced at Morales. "Give him a sample, just to make sure."

Morales instantly stepped in and swung a leather-covered fist at Clayburn's jaw. Clayburn side-stepped, dodging the punch. But then the two men behind him had hold of his upper arms, gripping him tightly, holding him in place. Clayburn didn't put up much of a struggle. There was nothing to be gained by it. Struggling would only postpone the inevitable by a matter of minutes. He was going to take a beating. The only thing he could control was the amount of punishment he would take, and there was only one way of doing that.

Morales spread his feet, grinned into Clayburn's face, and drove a huge fist into the hard muscles of Clayburn's middle. Clayburn was abruptly sick, sagging in the grip of the hands holding him, his legs giving way under him. He fought down the instinct to drive a bootheel into Morales' stomach. His head came up slowly, his eyes fastening on Morales. Eyes with no expression in them at all. He seemed merely to be memorizing Morales' features, riveting his face in his mind so he would never forget.

Morales' grin widened, showing his teeth. He drew back a fist and got all his bulk behind it as he swung, clubbing Clayburn across the side of the jaw. Clayburn's vision blurred and there seemed to be a rushing of dark waters through his brain.

Morales slammed another round-house punch into Clayburn's stomach. Clayburn became dead weight in the hands of the men holding him up. A low, grating sound trickled through his clenched teeth. Through a red haze he saw Morales driving the next punch at his mouth. Clayburn twisted his head and ducked, deliberately taking the sledgehammer blow full against his right temple, bracing himself to absorb the entire force of it.

There was an explosion inside Clayburn's skull. He drowned in darkness. . . .

The Texan finished watering the horses and strolled out of the stable. Shielding his eyes against the blazing afternoon sun, he glanced up at the church bell tower, where one of his men was on lookout. Then he looked toward where the other lookout was stationed—near the main gateway, the most likely approach for anyone coming into Arizeda. There was no sign from either lookout that anyone was in sight.

He headed across the dusty patio toward one of the inner doorways of what had once been a rich man's hacienda. His movements were quick and nervous. This wasn't the kind of job he relished. He needed savage, violent action to feel fully alive. Waiting and marking time had never been one of his strong points.

But it would be worth the waiting if Juan Ramirez did show up tomorrow. Otero's bonus for the delivery of Ramirez would weigh heavy in the pocket, even cut five ways. And that bonus would be doubled if he was delivered alive, so information about the rest of the rebels could be tortured out of him.

Personally, the Texan had a nagging doubt about whether the man they'd captured had been telling the truth. But by the following evening they'd know. And if Juan Ramirez didn't come. . . .

The Texan crossed a burnt-adobe walk and entered a huge, bare, high-ceilinged room. Morales and the squat, bearded man were using their saddles as chairs as they finished their mid-day beans and coffee near the huge open fireplace. Across the room Clayburn still lay on the floor with his back against the wall, his ankles roped together and his wrists tied behind him.

The Texan scowled at Clayburn's slack, unconscious face. Clayburn's temple was swollen, and there was a dark bruise covering most of one side of his jaw. His chest rose and fell slowly and heavily with his harsh breathing.

The bearded man glanced up at the Texan, then over toward Clayburn. ''He's still out.''

''I can *see* that,'' the Texan said irritably. ''Dammit, Morales, you got to take it a little easy with those fists of yours. You can't make a man talk by killing him.''

Morales grinned. ''He won't die . . . yet.''

''He better not,'' the Texan snapped. ''He's got a lot more talking to do—if Juan Ramirez don't show up.''

''Think he was lying to us?'' the bearded man asked.

"I don't know. . . . We'll find that out tomorrow."

Morales finished the last of his coffee, set the tin cup on the floor, and heaved to his feet. He trudged across the room and gazed down at the man lying on the floor. After a moment he drew back one foot and kicked Clayburn in the chest.

Clayburn's body rolled limply with the kick, the back of his shoulder bumping against the wall behind him, his head rolling loosely. There was a slight quiver in the muscles of his lean cheeks, a brief alteration in the pattern of his breathing.

Morales nodded, satisfied. "He will wake up before long."

The Texan continued to look down at the slack, unconscious face, studying it. He admitted to himself that it didn't look like the face of a dying man.

Turning to Morales, he said, "Time for you to relieve Mason up in the bell tower so he can eat." He looked at the bearded man. "You get out and take over from Ryan."

Morales got his carbine and went out. After the other man followed Morales, the Texan looked down at Clayburn again, observing his breathing. Then he went to the fireplace and poured some coffee in one of the tin cups. He was taking his first sip when there was a sound behind him.

The Texan turned quickly, his free hand reaching for his holstered gun—just in case. Clayburn was stirring fitfully, his bound legs drawing up a little, then straightening out again. His head raised up a fraction, fell, then jerked up a bit higher. The Texan took his hand from his gun, put down the cup, and crossed the room to stand over Clayburn, watching him with interest.

Clayburn's legs moved again, aimlessly. He moaned faintly. After a second, his eyes slitted open, closed, then opened again. Dazed, pain-filled eyes.

"Can you hear me?" the Texan growled.

Clayburn turned his head, winced. He squinted up at the Texan, but didn't seem able to focus on him clearly.

"Can you hear me?" the Texan repeated, louder.

The tip of Clayburn's tongue crept out and touched at his dry lips. His eyelids drooped shut. But he nodded, weakly.

"Then hear me good. What you're feeling right now's just a sample. If Juan Ramirez ain't here tomorrow, I'm gonna turn Morales loose on you again. And next time he ain't gonna hit you in the head at all. He'll just keep pounding away at your guts till they bust wide open and fill up with blood inside. Ever see a man die that way?"

Clayburn's eyes slitted open again. He moved his head cautiously, gritting his bared teeth against the pain.

"You still got a chance to change your story," the Texan told him. "Your last chance. Were you lying, before?"

Sound rattled in Clayburn's throat. His lips moved, and he whispered something through his teeth.

But it wasn't loud enough for the Texan to make out the words. He squatted beside Clayburn. "What was that?" He leaned closer to hear.

Clayburn's shoulders twitched. The Texan caught a blurred glimpse of Clayburn's arms flashing into view in front of him, the severed ropes falling away from his wrists.

Then Clayburn's left hand was clamped on the back of the Texan's neck like a vise, holding him down while the right fist jerked upward with five inches of slim, razor-sharp knife protruding from it.

The Texan's hand was closed around the grip of his holstered gun when the point of the knife ripped into him, just below the breastbone. His wild scream was cut short as the entire length of the cold steel explored his insides to the hilt and twisted expertly, severing everything it encountered.

SEVEN

The Texan's limp body rolled heavily across Clayburn's hips. His face froze in the expression with which he died; eyes wide and startled, mouth twisted in its silenced cry of agony.

Clayburn snatched the gun from the dead man's holster with his left hand. He rolled the body off him, jerking the knife out, dripping blood. With a grunt, he heaved himself to a sitting position, his slitted eyes on the doorway and two windows looking out on the patio, his finger across the trigger.

That death-scream was certain to have been heard.

With abrupt, painful effort, Clayburn bent forward and slashed at the ropes binding his ankles. His wrists were bleeding. It had taken him an hour of steadily rubbing them back and forth within the tight bite of the rope to work the knife hilt down to where the fingers of his left hand could get hold of it. Another half hour to saw through the rope.

But it only took seconds to cut the rope from his ankles. Quickly, still watching the door and windows, he slipped the knife back into the soft buckskin sheath strapped inside his left sleeve, and transferred the Colt to his right hand. Then he began the job of standing up.

It wasn't easy. The muscles across his middle felt like they'd been hacked to shreds and then sewed back together with barbed wire. His insides churned sickeningly when he moved, and a hammer seemed to be trying to drive a nail through his brain.

He finally got his feet under him and shoved himself up-

ward, swaying dizzily. He took a step and fell, landing hard
on both knees. Cursing viciously and softly, he forced himself to his feet again. And this time he stayed up. As the
dizziness ebbed, he began moving sideways toward an inner
doorway, gripping the Texan's Colt tightly in his right fist,
ready to fire at anything that moved.

But none of the other four men showed anywhere. And
there was no sound from any of them to indicate where they
were; or what they were doing.

Clayburn edged through the inner doorway, found himself
in a vaulted corridor leading out of the other side of the
house. Moving swiftly through it, he paused just inside the
doorway at the other end, looking out into the sunlight. There
was an open square out there, and on the other side of it was
a broken-down section of the town's outer wall. Through the
gaping hole in the wall he could see huge boulders and stone
spires and beyond them the looming wall of the cliff that
flanked Arizeda.

Clayburn edged forward a few more inches in the doorway, studying the buildings to his right. No one was in sight.
But he could see the bell tower of the church over the roofs,
which meant that if anyone was still up there they'd be able
to see him as soon as he was out in the open.

There was the sound of stamping horses to his left. Clayburn darted a look in that direction, saw an ancient stable
with part of the near wall missing. He hesitated, but not for
long. His chances of getting clear of the other four men were
dribbling away with each second he gave them to tighten a
net around him.

Launching himself out of the doorway, Clayburn sprinted
in a crouch toward the stable. A rifle blasted from the church
tower, the bullet kicking up dust two feet in front of him.
Clayburn dove forward, landed in the dust on his side, rolled
fast, and came up inside the ruins of the stable. He rose to
his feet with the Colt ready in his fist, seeing the horses in
front of him and the wide-open stable door to his left. Hearing the roar of an unseen rifle somewhere outside the doorway. Feeling the wind-whip of the bullet as it slashed past
his face.

He wasted no time trying to fire back at a rifleman he couldn't see. Grabbing for the horse that was nearest, he ripped loose its hitch-rope. He vaulted onto its back and raked it savagely with his bootheels, racing out of the stable the way he came in.

The next instant he was crossing the open square, hunched low over the pounding horse, heading for the break in the town wall with rifles blasting at him from several directions. Then he was through the wall, threading amongst the boulders outside, angling toward the broken cliff wall. There was only one rifle firing now, from the bell tower.

Glancing back, Clayburn saw three of the men sprinting from the town to the maze of boulders behind him. Each carried a rifle, and none was Morales. Which meant it was Morales up in that bell tower, firing down at him, each shot carefully spaced.

He was almost to the cliff when a bullet slashed down past his head and into the horse's skull between its ears. The horse lurched sideways and toppled over. Clayburn flung himself off as the animal went down. He landed on his feet, running. A bullet kicked a gout of clay against his boots. Then he was behind a boulder, crouching low so that Morales wouldn't be able to sight him from up in that bell tower. Dragging air into his lungs, he darted a look behind him. The other three men were hidden now among the other boulders.

Turning slightly, he studied the land around him, decided his best chance lay in a deep dry-gully running down from the base of the cliff.

Rifles roared from among the boulders as he sprinted into view—going away from the gully. He got a towering stone spire between him and the riflemen, spun around, and raced back out into the open the way he'd come. The trick bought him about two seconds in the clear. The riflemen had expected him to emerge from behind the spire going in the opposite direction. By the time they switched aim, Clayburn was vanishing behind a high outcropping of rock above the gully.

Flattening himself against the outcropping, he peered around its edge, watching the boulders. It was quiet now.

They'd begin moving out from their positions soon, circling to get him in sight. Not having a rifle of his own stacked the odds against him. They'd try to reach vantage points just beyond the short range of his hand gun. So they could cut him down with their rifles—if he held still for it.

Something flitted across the narrow space between two boulders. Clayburn didn't fire. He didn't want to warn them not to get that close to the Colt he held. Not yet. Shifting position, he launched himself around the edge of the out-cropping. A single rifle cracked. The bullet chopped flying splinters of rock against his cheek, drawing blood. Before another could be fired he was gone from sight, dropping down into the dry gully below him.

It was a long time since any rain water had run down off the cliff. The gully bottom was deep powdery sand with clumps of ocotillo and strawberry cactus growing up out of it. Clayburn ploughed his way upward with his boots sinking ankle keep in the sand, bending forward and down to keep his head below the gully walls.

A slab-sided boulder had toppled off the cliff and plunged into the gully, jamming it from side to side. He slapped his left hand down on top of the boulder and vaulted over it sideways, scraping his belt buckle across the top. He came down in a crouch on the other side and leaned against the boulder, panting.

It was about ten seconds since he'd dropped into the gully. Whipping off his hat, Clayburn wiped sweat from his eyes and tilted his head, straightening his knees slowly until he could see over the top of the boulder with one eye. Just as he did, one of his pursuers appeared below, at the mouth of the gully. Again Clayburn held his fire. The man threw him-self down in the instant of showing himself, rolled swiftly and vanished. It had been a feint, to make him waste bullets and reveal his exact position. They weren't amateurs at this. But neither was Clayburn.

He backed away from the boulder, climbing higher up the gully, watching for one of them to show himself again. The way became steeper as he got higher up the base of the cliff.

But the rock rubble here formed a series of broken, uneven steps that helped.

It was where the gully began to shallow out that he found what he needed: a crevice in the broken wall of the cliff, big enough for a man to fit into. Clayburn dropped to the ground and shoved himself backward into the dark shadow of the crevice in a sitting position. Now he had solid rock protecting his back and sides, and a jutting overhang concealing him from above. And he was now beyond range of Morales in the bell tower. Drawing his legs up into the shadow of the crevice, he settled down to wait. Resting both forearms on his knees, both hands steadying the gun aimed at the boulder over which anyone would have to come to climb the gully after him.

Silent minutes dragged by. Clayburn stayed where he was, motionless, part of the rocks and shadows, his insides tight as a drawn bow-string.

The dark crown of a hat edged up into view over the other side of the boulder Clayburn was watching. His finger tensed across the trigger, but he did not fire.

The hat stayed in view for almost half a minute, then was lowered out of sight. A moment later the top of a hatless head jerk up into sight, just enough for an eye to take a quick peek over the top of the boulder. Just as abruptly, the head ducked back down behind the boulder.

Clayburn waited. There was a sleepy glitter in his eyes.

The head came up again, more slowly this time, and higher. It was the squat, bearded man. He raised up enough for both eyes to search the upper gully. The sights of the Colt in Clayburn's hands were lined up with the exact center of the man's forehead. But he continued to wait.

The bearded man took his time, looking. But he did not see Clayburn in the dark shadow of the rock cleft. Finally, he began hauling himself up over the boulder, his eyes still searching warily, a carbine held ready to fire in his right hand.

That carbine was what Clayburn had been waiting for. As the bearded man swung himself across the top of the boulder, Clayburn shifted his sights to the man's body. The distance was chancey for his hand gun, but an easy shot for the other man's weapon. He couldn't afford to miss with the first one.

The bearded man dropped to his spread feet on the near side of the boulder, swiftly bringing up the carbine in both hands. Clayburn's finger tightened. The Colt roared, bucking against the heel of his palm. The bullet tore the other man's side, the force of it spinning him around. He staggered for balance, trying to bring his carbine to bear on Clayburn's revealed position. Clayburn fired twice more in rapid succession, the blast of the shots blending together, echoing harshly off the rock formations of the cliff wall.

Both of the heavy .45 slugs drummed into the bearded man's broad chest, hammering him backward off his feet, slamming him to the ground. His legs bent convulsively, straightened, and then were still.

Clayburn crouch-sprinted down the gully. His long, rope-scarred fingers made quick work of unbuckling the dead man's gunbelt, yanking it out from under the body. Jamming the Colt he'd used down inside his pants, he made it back up to the rock cleft with the gunbelt in one hand and the carbine in his other.

Strapping the gunbelt around his hips, he settled down within the protection of the rock cleft again, in the same position as before. But with a difference. The difference being the carbine he now held ready in his hands. It wasn't only the greater range of the carbine. Even at shorter ranges, Clayburn preferred a rifle. It was a more dependable weapon, for anything except close-up, point-blank work.

The carbine made him feel better about the hours ahead till dusk. With it, he didn't think they'd be able to get at him in daylight. And if he could survive until night, he was quite sure he could get away in the dark.

"Benjy?" one of the other men called from somewhere down the gully.

So now the bearded man crumpled under the boulder had a name. The call was not repeated. Benjy hadn't answered, and the reason would be obvious. The other two down there wouldn't be anxious to follow him over that boulder. Clayburn waited; watching, listening. . . .

Half an hour went by with no sign or sound from them. Clayburn's tension began to slacken a little. Enough for him to become increasingly aware of the aching of his head, the pain in his middle.

Shadows lengthened across the glare-lit land outside his rock cleft. Thirst added itself to his other discomforts, needling his tongue, the inside of his dry throat. Swallowing became difficult. Clayburn toyed with the possibility that they might have pulled out . . .

A small stone clattered down the overhang above him, dropped past the shadowed cleft, and plunked to the ground inches beyond his drawn-in boots.

Clayburn instantly shifted the carbine, looking upward. One of them was up there, trying to get down at him from above.

There was a period of silence after the falling of the stone. Then Clayburn heard the faint scrape of a bootheel across the stone of the overhang. He waited, all of him tensed for the quick-aim and trigger squeeze. The sound was not repeated. Nothing appeared.

Keeping the carbine tilted upward, Clayburn darted a glance down the gully. There was no one in sight there, either. His eyes moved upward again. There was no way the man on the overhang could shoot at him without exposing himself. But there were other things the man could do from up there—like dropping burning brush to smoke him out of the cleft. . . .

A gun boomed somewhere above.

There was a metallic skittering across stone and a Colt revolver fell beside the little stone. Something else came sliding and rolling down the overhang. Something heavy, and not metallic. One of the men who'd trapped him in the town spilled over the lip of the overhang. He hit the bottom of the gully on his side and sprawled over loosely on his belly, his face sinking deep into the soft sand. He didn't lift his face out of the sand. The back of his head had been blown off.

From down the gully came the sound of someone running. Running away.

From somewhere above a man called down, "You can come out now, Clay. You're among friends."

Clayburn recognized the voice. Brazos Williams—a lean, leathery, ageless wrangler who'd worked for Diego Ramirez on both sides of the border as far back as he could remember.

Shoving up out of the rock cleft, Clayburn spared one swift look upward at the figure of Brazos, standing atop the cliff wall with a rifle in his hands. Then he stepped over the body of the man Brazos had killed and went down the gully to where the bearded man lay. Looking over the top of the slab-sided boulder there, he caught a glimpse of the third man running toward the abandoned town, flitting from one boulder to the next.

Clayburn slid his carbine across the top of the boulder and waited, aiming at the open space between the boulders and the town wall, intending to get the running man when he emerged into that open space.

But the man didn't get that far. He appeared suddenly from behind a pile of rocks, sprinting toward a stone spire. There was a double gun-roar to his right. He was flung sideways against a boulder, his rifle spilling from his hands. Sliding down the boulder, he sank to his knees, bending forward with his head almost touching dirt, both hands trying to stop the blood pumping out of his stomach.

A slim, handsome young Mexican of medium height stepped out from behind another boulder. His clothes were those of a vaquero—but even the dust could not hide their expensive quality. He dangled a pistol carelessly in each hand. Walking over to the gun-shot man, he looked down and said something that didn't carry to Clayburn.

The kneeling man raised his head slowly, looking up. His lips moved. The young Mexican smiled, showing very white teeth. He raised one of his pistols and placed its muzzle between the kneeling man's eyes, and put a bullet in his brain.

Walking around the man's crumpled figure, he started up toward the gully. Clayburn swung over the boulder and went down to meet him. "There's another inside the town," he said in Spanish.

"Only one?"

"His name's Morales."

"Morales? . . . Ah!" The slim Mexican looked toward the town.

At that moment, two saddled horses broke out through a gap in the wall on the other side of the town and raced together up the far slope toward a thick-wooded notch in the gorge. The figure of Morales could barely be seen, hanging down between the two horses. They were halfway up the slope when rifle-shots sounded, from another wooded section on the far side. Three shots, one after another.

One of the horses faltered and went down. Morales pulled himself up into the saddle of the other horse, hunching down low as he spurred it up toward the notch. Clayburn stared to raise his carbine, but lowered it. The distance was too great.

But not too great for the rifleman firing along the opposite slope. There were two more shots. The horse staggered and fell sideways. Morales thudded to the ground beside it, leaped up, and sprinted the rest of the way to the notch. The hidden rifle cracked twice more, missing both times. Morales made it into the notch afoot, and disappeared.

The handsome young Mexican beside Clayburn cursed softly in Spanish.

"Your man is a pretty good shot," Clayburn said dryly. "But not good enough."

"Perhaps. But Gila has his uses—being half Apache."

The rifleman, Gila, appeared on the opposite slope, riding a black horse. He looked toward the notch, then across toward the young Mexican and Clayburn. The Mexican raised his arm high and motioned the rider in.

"It is a shame to lose Morales," he said, scowling toward the notch and appearing to be speaking mostly to himself. "But where he has gone there are many places for a man to hide, and night comes soon. We might not find him until late tomorrow, and it is not wise to stay here that long. Some of Dietrich's force may have discovered our trail and be coming this way."

He turned his head and gave Clayburn his full attention for a moment, looking him over thoughtfully. "Well, Señor

Clayburn, I have heard interesting things about you. From Brazos Williams. And from my sister. . . . She seems to find you especially interesting.''

Clayburn had heard he was young. But with the amount of slaughter and looting that went with the name, he hadn't expected anyone that looked quite this young. And innocent.

''You're Latigo?''

The other smiled at him. Much in the way he had smiled at the gut-shot man before putting a bullet through his brain. ''But of course.''

EIGHT

In the starlit darkness of the deep ravine, Clayburn sat loosely with his back resting against a cottonwood stump, sleepily finishing a last smoke while Latigo pondered the news he'd brought from Juan. Brazos and Gila were out of sight on opposite rims of the ravine, taking the first half of the night watch. Serina lay on the grass near Clayburn and Latigo, apparently already sound asleep in the roll of her blanket. Despite what her brother had said about her interest in him she'd shown no evidence of it, almost studiously ignoring his presence all the way from Arizeda.

They'd ridden south from Arizeda, across a sun-blasted land of sage, creosote and sparse yuccas, into a country of looming mesas and jagged buttes and alkali dust. Stopping only briefly for a meal rest at sundown, then pushing on through the darkness.

They had no way of knowing whether Dietrich and his men were on their trail or not, and weren't taking any chances.

It had been Serina, approaching Arizeda from the border, who'd spotted the dust of Dietrich's riders coming, in time to warn the rebel band waiting there for Juan. They'd all fled from the town and managed to get away into the mountains, far enough ahead of Dietrich to stay ahead. But that had still left the problem of Juan Ramirez, who was expecting to make contact with them at Arizeda.

So once into the mountains, Latigo had detached himself from the bulk of the rebel band, taking Serina, Brazos and

Gila with him. They'd holed up behind cover, let Dietrich's gang go past them following the trail left by the others, and then begun circling back toward Arizeda.

With Juan as badly hurt as Serina had reported, they hadn't expected to find him there so soon. But Latigo was taking no chances. He'd intended to check Arizeda, just to make sure, and then head north, splitting his small party to the few trails Juan would be most likely to use when he did come south.

It was not that Latigo cared about Juan's welfare. Clayburn got the impression Latigo would like nothing better than being able to take over complete leadership of the rebellion, in the event of Juan's death. But the rebellion needed the arms and ammunition Juan had gone north to arrange for. And only Juan knew about that arrangement, including such vital facts as time and place of delivery.

Latigo's small group had been nearing Arizeda when they'd heard the sound of shooting coming from it. Gila had been sent on a swing around the gorge to have a look at the town from one side. Latigo and Brazos had crept toward the other side, leaving their horses with Serina. It had been Brazos, peering over the rim of the cliff through fieldglasses, who'd spotted Clayburn making his way up the gully. And recognized him. . . .

As soon as Clayburn had informed Latigo that Juan would not be coming to Arizeda when he was able to travel, they'd headed south. And kept going until almost midnight, when they'd come to this place. Gila had been the one who'd known of this ravine with the fresh-water spring in its depths, and had led them to it.

For Clayburn, it had been worth the trip. Crushing out the stub of his cigarette under his heel, he leaned back and savored the relative cool of the night, the trickling of the spring, the restoring smell of cottonwood leaves and damp grass.

Latigo suddenly raised his head, pulling himself out of his troubling thoughts as he turned toward Clayburn. "Getting word to Ramirez at Oputo is no problem," he said slowly. "I will send Brazos there to wait until he comes, and tell him where to find us. But the money for the Winchesters and ammunition . . . that is not so easy.''

"Juan said you've already got some of it."

"Far from the full amount. We need almost twenty-one thousand American dollars more to meet that price. If *you* have any ideas about how we can get our hands on so much. . . ."

"I'd say the answer's obvious," Clayburn said dryly. "Especially for you."

"You mean steal it. But there is nothing in this country to steal. Dietrich and Otero have already picked it clean. Looted all the big haciendas and the towns of everything—gold, silver, money, jewels. What little some people were able to hide from them, they have already given willingly to Juan Ramirez to help. There is nothing left—except cattle, horses, sheep. . . . But these are too slow to transport north for sale. We would be caught before we reached the border.''

Latigo was silent for a moment, going over the possibilities in his mind. "There are the silver mines, of course. But they are too heavily guarded for our small force. And Otero will move no silver trains from them until we are wiped out. . . .

"I have considered raiding north of the border again for it. But so much money . . . no single bank close to the border carries that much. It would take time to get it, and with the American army on our heels all the way, to say nothing of every lawman in. . . .''

"I still say the answer is obvious," Clayburn cut in. "Take it from the ones who've got it. Where does Otero keep all that loot he's seized?"

Latigo grinned at him. "You have the makings of a good thief, Señor Clayburn. But that presents a problem. You see, Otero keeps all of it at his headquarters in the old fortress in Losquadros Canyon.''

"That does present a problem."

"You know Losquadros?"

"I've been there."

"But not recently. It is not only the enormous number of men who guard Losquadros for Otero. Dietrich has made it impossible for even a single unauthorized man to get in there armed. Equally impossible to get out again.'' Latigo told him about the precautions taken by Dietrich.

Clayburn considered them, and what he remembered of Losquadros. Finally he said, "There's still one possible way to get out. A dangerous way, but. . . ." He told Latigo what he had in mind.

Latigo shook his head. "I have thought of that. As you say, very dangerous. Perhaps impossible. Only one man has gotten out alive through that route. Yet I would try it except—have you got any idea how much over twenty thousand dollars worth of gold and silver would weigh?''

''I was thinking about jewelry. If Otero's got the jewelry taken from every rich family in this part of Sonora, that alone ought to be worth enough. And twenty thousand dollars worth of jewelry can be carried quite easily.''

Latigo grinned at him again. And shook his head again. ''You do have the mind of a thief. This too has been considered. It was with such a thing in mind that I had one of my own men join Dietrich's mercenaries. Joe Fenton. Perhaps you have heard of him?''

Clayburn nodded. Joe Fenton had gotten himself a reputation for shooting men in the back when he had been working as a gunhawk for one side in the Mercer County cattle war in Texas. Fenton preferred the safer way of doing things, when possible. Not that anyone doubted his guts because of it. He'd followed up his Mercer County stint by pulling a string of single-handed bank and stage robberies across Arizona and New Mexico. Two years back things had finally gotten too hot for him north of the border, and he'd vanished into Mexico.

''I've heard of him.''

''Then you know his capabilities. But Fenton has been with Dietrich for almost five weeks now, much of that time spent in Losquadros—and he has been unable to get anywhere near the place where Otero has the treasure stored. And if he cannot even get there to steal. . . .''

''Maybe *I* can,'' Clayburn said quietly.''

Latigo stared at him. "You?''

"Me. If Joe Fenton was able to join up with Dietrich, I should be able to. Especially with him already a member, so he can recommend me for the job."

"Do you really think you can do what a man of Fenton's experience has not succeeded in. . . ?"

Clayburn was thinking, not so much about the jewelry, as about the opportunity to get that close to Dietrich. "It's worth a try. . . ."

Suddenly, surprisingly, Serina spoke from her blanket roll. "You are a big fool, Clayburn."

The two men looked at her, startled. Latigo snapped, "Be quiet, sister! This is nothing you understand."

Serina sat up, looking at Clayburn. It was impossible to make out the expression on her night-shadowed face. "I understand foolishness when I hear it. Dietrich has two men who know you are with Juan Ramirez."

"Morales is a long way north, on foot," Clayburn told her. "It'll take him time to get a horse and reach Losquadros."

"And what about Hogan?"

"I told you to be quiet," her brother warned her.

"I don't intend to go in there if either Hogan or Morales is around to identify me," Clayburn told her patiently. "There's Fenton, already planted in Dietrich's gang, to let us know when it's safe. I'll go in when neither of them is there. And try to get out before either of them shows up."

"And suppose your luck runs out while you are there?" Serina pointed out thinly. "Suppose one of them comes back while you are still trapped inside. . . ."

Latigo slapped her across the face, hard. It rocked her, and for an instant Clayburn thought she was going to strike back.

She didn't, but Clayburn was quite sure it wasn't fear that held her back. In Mexico a man was supposed to be able to control his womenfolk; with force when words failed. And Latigo was Serina's brother. It was a point of family pride, for her as well as him.

Clayburn smiled at her. "I appreciate your concern for me, but. . . ."

"Who cares what happens to you?" she cut in acidly. "It is the danger to our cause I was thinking of. But if you *both* think I am too stupid to listen to. . . ." She wrapped the blanket around her and lay down again, turning her back to them.

Clayburn was reminded of the other time she'd done that, on his bed in Tubavi Springs. . . .

"If *you* are willing to take the risk. . . ." Latigo said slowly.

Clayburn forced his eyes away from Serina's motionless, shadowed figure and said flatly, "I'm not willing to take *any* risks that we can do something about."

For a time they quietly discussed what could be done about those risks. Then they both stretched out to get some sleep. Clayburn knew exactly how thin a chance he was taking. But he knew also that he *was* going to take it—and that it would be sensible to get as much rest as possible inside him beforehand. A man who'd lived the life he had, learned to store up sleep whenever he could; no matter what was plucking at his nerves. Shutting his eyes and deliberately blanking everything out of his mind, he drifted into darkness. . . .

He awoke exactly three hours later. And was not surprised to see Latigo rise from the ground at the same time he did. Silently, with no need for words between them, they headed away from the spring, separating to climb opposite slopes of the ravine.

Clayburn found Brazos Williams sitting against a cut of rock, gazing off across the distances. Coming up beside him soundlessly, he said, "Your turn for sleep."

Brazos jumped, grabbing for the rifle across his knees. Then he relaxed. "Damn! You always did walk like a cat— or an Injun. . . ." He stood up stiffly. "Nothin' moving out there. Have an interestin' talk with Latigo?"

Clayburn nodded. "Interesting."

"What d'you think of the boy?" Brazos asked dryly, his leathery, ageless face expressionless.

"Interesting. . . ." Clayburn smiled a small smile. "Like a tarantula's interesting."

"Yeah. . . . That boy's tough, make no mistake about that.

And pure mean clear through. You know what he's in this for, don't you?''

"For himself."

"Damn right. Figures he can get to be a big man in the power scramble that'll come if General Otero falls."

"What happens afterwards doesn't concern me," Clayburn said.

"Sure. . . . That's the way I see it, too. But watch out for him, Clay. You better watch him real close. And those characters he brought in with him.''

''I figure to,'' Clayburn told him.

Brazos started down the slope toward the spring, nothing about the way he moved showing his age. Across the ravine, Clayburn saw Gila working his way down the other slope. The stocky, vicious-looking half-Apache had not had much to say all the way from Arizeda. He'd been sulking about having let Morales get away from him. Clayburn pitied the next man Gila went up against.

Turning from the ravine, Clayburn spent a long time scanning the surrounding country. Then he leaned against the cut of rock and gazed south, across the moonlit mesas and long-shadowed buttes to the dark horizon. Thinking about an old man named Diego Ramirez; a tough, decent man who'd taken in an orphaned boy and treated him like his own. Thinking about a man named Dietrich, waiting in Losquadros.

NINE

A horned lizard panted in the thin shade of a sandstone butte that had been pitted by hundreds of years of winds until it looked like a sponge. The lizard did not move when the horse appeared circling around the scalding steam hissing out of a ground vent, coming to a halt a few feet away to share the butte's protecting shade. For about five minutes the horse remained there, motionless as the lizard. Then its rider kicked it, forcing the horse out again into the remorseless sunlight. Out across the barren, flat, scorched land that lay like a vast frying pan that had been burned to a black crust from being left too long over a fire.

Clayburn angled past the butte toward the looming blue of the mountain range. He rode with a neckerchief tied over his lower face, to protect his nostrils from the clouds of acrid lava dust stirred up by the plodding hooves of his sorrel horse. The heat of the boiling springs underground rose up to meet the heat pushing down from a cloudless, yellowish sky. It was like riding through the inside of a bake oven.

He rode alone. Brazos had struck out for Oputo to wait for Juan. Serina had started for Losquadros five hours earlier, to make contact with Joe Fenton before Clayburn arrived. Latigo and Gila would follow the next day. Clayburn would have preferred to go in at night, when there would be less chance of being recognized if either Morales or Hogan was around. But no one without a permit was allowed to enter Otero's stronghold by night; just one of Dietrich's precautions. So Clayburn paced himself to arrive just before dusk.

What would happen in the time between entering and getting under cover was in the hands of the fates.

Leaving the lava flats behind him at last, he rode up into a country created long before man by the violent upheaving and spewing-forth of now-dead volcanoes. He went up into the mountains past smooth hills of lava rock and over hardened black lava flows, threading around gigantic craters pushing up toward the sky. It was afternoon when he finally entered the Canyon del Losquadros.

A river had once run down this way from the core of the mountain range, grooving this deep trench in the solid rock. But it was thousands of years since the river had flowed this far. Now there was nothing in the lower stretch of the canyon but stone, sand and clay; its depths barren except for sparse growths of mesquite, clumps of broomweed, an occasional flame-tipped candlewood.

Clayburn followed the course of the canyon as it wound upward through the heart of the mountains that were the remains of the prehistoric volcanoes. An hour before dusk the bottom of the canyon began to become less barren. The first hint was brought by the sudden appearance of a few birds flitting overhead. Then the vegetation became gradually less sparse, more varied. Sage grew along the base of the canyon walls; flowering shrubs, brush, organ-pipe cactus; a thicket of yuccas gave way to stunted junipers.

The sorrel horse increased its pace without urging, smelling water ahead. Clayburn went around a sharp, hairpin bend. He heard it before he saw it: the Losquadros River, rushing down the mountains through another branch of the canyon. Following its downward course, he entered another world. A fertile green world of lush grass and fields of flowers and thick stands of pine.

Clayburn pulled the neckerchief down from his face, instinctively drawing a deep breath of relief as he rode a well-worn path between the river bank and the right wall of the canyon, filling his dust-dry lungs with the fresh, moistened air.

The sense of relief was short-lived. Something that had not been here the last time he'd come this way lay dead ahead of him, across his path: a low stone wall. On top of this wall stood half a dozen of Otero's soldiers, their faces shadowed by their wide-brimmed, high-pointed sombreros; their hands holding rifles on him as he approached.

Clayburn kept on toward them without pausing, looking at them and what lay behind them as he drew nearer. Beyond the new stone wall the canyon widened—and ended. It was a vast box canyon, completely surrounded by red cliffs that rose straight and sheer for over a thousand feet; impossible to climb, up or down. There was only one way into this box: the route Clayburn was using; the route carved through solid rock by the river.

Beyond the stone wall the river flowed through lush little farms with their herds of goats, grassy slopes with their fat cattle; past the village, past the old, solid fortress. And then the river disappeared—plunging into a hole in the rear cliff wall, pouring down into the volcano-riddled depths under the mountains.

Once this boxed-in area had been a high trapped lake, before it had unplugged itself through that hole. It had left behind the rich, thick layer of sediment for the farms and pasture that supported the people of the village—and now fed the troops of the fortress of Losquadros. That, plus the absolute protection of the surrounding towering cliffs, made this a perfect headquarters for Otero and Dietrich.

The red of those cliffs was turning the color of dark blood in the sunset when Clayburn rode through the opened gate in the stone wall across the entrance into the box canyon. A uniformed officer stood blocking his way on the other side of the wall. Clayburn reined the sorrel to a halt. There were more armed men on either side of him. Morales and Hogan were not among them. Clayburn made sure of that before he obeyed the officer's gesture, swinging down to the ground.

"You have a permit from General Otero?" the officer demanded.

"No. Just passing through. Thought I'd lay up here for a couple days." There was nothing odd about the explanation. The Canyon del Losquadros was a natural, much-used route to the more fertile and populated country on the other side of the mountains.

"Then you will have to leave all your weapons here," the officer told him. "They will be returned to you when you leave."

Clayburn nodded and unbuckled his gunbelt. It was taken by a trooper, who also took his carbine, and the sheathed knife which Clayburn had transferred from his arm to his saddlebags before entering the canyon. Latigo had warned him not to try hiding anything; and that they would be thorough in searching him.

They were thorough. The officer ran practiced hands over every part of him. He was even ordered to take off his hat and boots so these could be examined, while another trooper went carefully through his saddle gear.

While they were at it, Clayburn observed everything around him without appearing to. And recorded what he observed, for future use. Three adobe shacks huddled against the base of the cliff at one end of the inner wall. Headquarters for the wall garrison. There were altogether fifteen men guarding the wall. But any force that managed to get past them would run right into five cannons that were lined up two hundred yards away—trained on the wall, the gate and the river. Artillery crews and a stack of iron balls were ready behind each cannon. Clayburn guessed that the cannons were already primed, and probably loaded with enough chain-shot to slash to ribbons any massed charge. The age of these old muzzle-loading pieces didn't mean that they couldn't be effective.

The search for concealed weapons over, Clayburn set his hat back on his head and tugged on his boots. As he mounted up and rode deeper into the widening box canyon, he heard the gate clanging shut behind him. Twilight was darkening within the sheer surrounding cliffs. Nobody else without a permit would be allowed to enter until the following morning. And no one would be allowed out.

He felt nakedly vulnerable as he followed the worn wagon road past the farms toward the village. If he ran into trouble now, he'd be trapped in here without anything to protect himself with. Tugging the front brim of his battered slouch hat lower to shadow his face as much as possible, he kept the sorrel to a very slow walk. Giving the murk of dusk time to thicken for some measure of concealment, his narrowed eyes took in every man within sight along the way.

In a small farmyard he passed, young goats were beginning to wander away from the little stone wall whose shade had protected them from the day's killing sun. A boy milking a she-goat glanced up at him and then quickly looked away, his face tight with fear and resentment. Any stranger might be working for Otero and Dietrich. It would be rough on these people, having that bunch quartered in here with them.

The road curved past an orange grove and entered the village. It cut between the rows of adobe-brick buildings whose walls ran one into the next, leading into a small, palm-shaded plaza. Clayburn didn't stay with it to the plaza. Instead he turned into the first alley on his right that he came to. Slipping down from the sorrel, he led it the rest of the way through the alley, between a high-walled wagon-yard and a blacksmith's shed. At the other end he angled left, away from a town pump where two women were filling their buckets, past the back of a leather shop and the side wall of a cantina. He entered the rear of a stable and came to a halt just inside, giving his eyes time to adjust to the dimness of its interior.

From the shadows in one corner a voice spoke: "You are late." Serina came quickly toward him from the shadows. "Come with me. Hogan is here."

Clayburn tensed. "In town?"

She nodded. "In the cantina, drinking."

"What about Morales?"

"About him, I don't know." She seized his hand. "Come. . . ."

"Got to take care of my horse first."

Serina turned her head and snapped: "Roa!"

A short, wiry Mexican stepped hesitantly out of the shadows along the wall. His frightened eyes didn't look at Clayburn as he took the reins and turned away without a word.

"Roa will tend to the horse." Serina tugged his hand impatiently. Clayburn went with her.

She took him through a small side door, into a narrow corridor in a house attached to the stable. At the end of the corridor a short flight of wooden brick steps led down to a low wooden door below ground level. Opening this door, Serina had to stoop as she went through it and was swallowed up by the pitch blackness inside. Clayburn waited. There was the flare of a match. Then the glow of a kerosene lamp, revealing a small, windowless cellar.

Clayburn bent down and went in, shutting the door behind him. The cellar was used as a storeroom. There were used-up farm tools, coils of new rope, a keg of nails, some packing boxes, a bureau with all its drawers missing, and other odds and ends. Against the wall were several straw-filled pallets on the hard clay floor. The dank cellar room had obviously been used as a hiding place before this.

Taking off his hat, Clayburn slapped it against his leg, knocking a cloud of dust from it. "Dietrich's bunch back yet?"

Serina set the lamp on the bureau and turned to him. "No. And Fenton is out with them. So we will have to wait until they come back to talk to him."

Clayburn scowled, threw his hat on a packing case. "How long's Hogan been back?"

"Since yesterday, Roa says."

"But nobody's seen Morales?"

"No. What do we do about Hogan?"

"I don't know yet," Clayburn told her. The quickest solution to the problem would be to lure Hogan into a dark alley, alone, kill him and bury his body. But that might stir up other problems. "I'll decide that after I've had a chance to talk with Joe Fenton. Right now I want to wash up."

Serina jerked a thumb at a far corner of the cellar. "The water is in the bucket there."

Clayburn started toward the bucket. "Go get me something to drink. Cold beer if you can. I'm full of dust inside, too."

"Do not order me around," Serina snapped. "I am not your servant. Or your—anything."

Clayburn looked at her. "I'm going to wash all over." He began to unbuckle the belt of his Levi's. "You can stay and watch, if you want to."

He grinned after her as she went out with an insolent flip of her hips. When the low door shut behind her, he stripped to the skin, slamming each item of clothing against the wall to knock the caked dust from it. Then he used the bucket of water to wash himself from head to toes, drawing an almost sensual pleasure from the cold wetness soaking into his parched flesh.

He took his time with it, and when he was done he used the buckskin shirt to blot some of the excess moisture from his body. Hanging the shirt on a wall hook to dry, he pulled on the Levi's. He was buckling the belt when Serina came back in with a bottle of beer.

Clayburn seized it from her hand, pulled the cork, and drank from it greedily. The beer wasn't cold, but cool enough to serve the purpose. Serina rested a hip on the edge of a packing box, watching him drink. Her dark eyes took in his heavy, sloping shoulders, his bared chest and lean middle. They observed the play of the flat, powerful back muscles as he lowered the bottle with a sigh of pleasure, then raised it to his mouth again. The tip of her tongue crept out to moisten her ripe lower lip. Otherwise nothing about her thoughtful, watchful expression changed.

Clayburn didn't set down the bottle until it was empty. He wiped the back of a hand across his hard mouth and grinned at her. "That's better. Now something to eat and I'll be able to think out what comes next."

"The food will be ready soon," she told him. And then, "I still think you are a fool to try this."

"*You* came here," he pointed out. "That was taking a chance on Hogan spotting you. And tomorrow your brother'll be taking his chances when he comes in. There must be a lot of people who know what he looks like."

"No one will recognize him. He will come with an oxcart, dressed like a peasant, his face covered with dust. He has done it before.''

"Your brother's got nerve," Clayburn conceded. Lowering himself to one of the straw pallets, he leaned back against the cool wall and stretched out his long legs. "For that matter, so do you."

She softened a little under the praise. "But we will not go into that fortress. . . ."

"Neither will I, as long as Hogan's around. The same goes for Morales." Clayburn got the makings from a pocket of his Levi's, began rolling a cigarette. "I didn't come down here to commit suicide."

"Why *did* you join us?"

"To settle a score."

She studied him a moment, thoughtfully. "And afterwards? If we win . . . and you are still alive?"

Clayburn lit the cigarette. "Afterwards—I'll go back where I belong." He shook out the match. "And you? What're your plans—for afterward?"

"If we beat Otero. . . ?" Her face got a dreamy look. "My life will be very different. My brother will be an outlaw no more. He will be an important man in this country. I will have beautiful clothes to wear; jewels, servants, a great hacienda. . . ."

Clayburn's smile was thin. "And a rich, respectable husband to go with it?"

Serina stiffened, fire flickering in her dark eyes. "Why not? You think it is impossible?"

Clayburn took a deep drag at the cigarette, let the smoke trickle out slowly. "All things are possible."

"I will be a good wife," she said flatly. "For the right man. I will be very loyal to the husband I choose. And give him much pleasure. . . ."

Clayburn's eyes took in her supple figure. "That part I'd bet on," he said softly.

Her laugh, too, was soft. She caught her lower lip between her teeth and stared at him in silence for a moment. Then she eased off the packing box and said, "I will get the meal for us now."

After she left, Clayburn took a last drag from the cigarette and stubbed it out on the floor. Then he locked his hands behind his head and leaned back against the wall, gazing up at the low ceiling with no expression at all.

Five minutes later Serina returned with two plates of tortillas and a bottle of tequila on a tray. And with her face alive with excitement. "Dietrich has returned with his men! I watched them ride past to the fortress!"

Clayburn lowered his arms and sat up straighter. "Fenton with them?"

She nodded. "Later many of the men will come from the fortress to enjoy themselves in town. In the cantinas and the house of women. . . . Fenton always comes too, and checks with Roa."

"Got any idea when he'll show up?"

Serina shrugged. "Sometime during the night."

"Nothing to do but wait, then. Let's have at that food."

Serina was too excited to eat much. But not Clayburn. He finished off his heaping plate of tortillas before she was a third of the way through hers. Washing the meal down with a jolt of the tequila, he stretched out on one of the pallets and shut his eyes.

Serina stared down at him. "You are going to sleep? *Now?*"

"Uh-huh," he murmured. "Now."

And he did.

TEN

Three hours later Serina was nervously pacing the cellar room, with irritated glances toward Clayburn sound asleep on his pallet, when there was a tapping at the door.

Serina was startled by the abruptness of Clayburn's response. Before she could fully turn toward the sound he was on his feet, no trace of sleepiness in his face. One moment he was stretched out dead to the world. The next he was reaching the wall beside the door in what seemed to be one smooth-flowing movement; gesturing for her to open up.

When she opened the door, Clayburn was hidden behind it. He heard a man with a deep gravelly voice: "H'lo, Serina. What's up?"

Serina pulled the man in and shut the door. "Fenton . . . this is Clayburn."

Joe Fenton swung around to face Clayburn, with a speed that belied the ungainly look of him. He was a bearlike, paunchy man in his middle forties, with a fat cheerful face suddenly frozen hard.

Serina said quickly: "Clayburn is working for my brother."

Clayburn didn't contradict her.

The hardness thawed out of Fenton's face. He grinned at Clayburn and stuck out a meaty hand. "Welcome to the party, friend."

Clayburn shook hands with him, remembering that Fenton was supposed to be left-handed. There were stories about Fenton anchoring a man's gun-hand this way, just long

71

enough to draw and shoot the other man. But Fenton wasn't
wearing any gun in sight. Which brought up a point.

Withdrawing his hand, Clayburn asked, "You don't happen to have a gun somewhere on you, that I could borrow
for a while?"

Fenton looked genuinely sorry not to be able to do a friend
that favor. "Nope. Dietrich don't let any of us carry guns
except when we're on duty. Figures there's bound to be some
fights, now and then, and he don't want us killing each other.
Careful guy, Dietrich."

He looked from Clayburn to Serina. "Tell me what's doing. I got a whiskey bottle and a hot brunette waiting for me
over at Dolores' place." We winked at Serina. "Unless
you're in the mood, honey. . . ."

Serina's stony scorn didn't faze him a bit.

Clayburn told him what he'd come for, and the problem
raised by the fact that Hogan and Morales knew him. Fenton
listened to all of it intently, not interrupting.

"Well, well. . . ." he murmured when Clayburn had finished. He scratched his jaw and thought about it. Finally he
said slowly, "About Hogan—relax. He had a talk with Dietrich and he's heading back north of the border first thing
tomorrow. Along with another of the boys named Seelig."

Clayburn's eyes narrowed. "What for?"

Fenton shrugged. "Who knows? Nobody tells me much.
All I know is, Seelig was up in Bisbee, looking for Juan
Ramirez. So maybe he found out something about what Ra-
mirez was up there for."

Clayburn tucked that away in the back of his mind, to be
thought about later. "What about Morales?"

"That's a good question. Nobody knows where he is. Not
here, that's for sure. After we lost the bunch we were trailing,
we turned back to Arizeda. Found the other ones dead, but not
Morales. And we didn't run into him on the way back here.
So I'd guess he was hiking it this way, by another route."

"That means I've got between tomorrow morning, when Hogan leaves, and whenever Morales arrives to get the job done."

Fenton nodded, his eyes going small at the thought. "Yeah.
And no way of telling *when* Morales'll show up. And if he

does while we're still in there—it'll be my neck, along with yours. Me being the one who brought you in.''

He scratched his jaw again, looking dubious. ''Having another man in there with me might help—if there was only some way to get near that treasure room. If we can't, it sure ain't worth the risk of bringing you in.''

''You know *where* the treasure's stored?''

''Oh, sure. But I ain't been able to get near enough to even look at it from the outside. It's got a special bunch of guards, separate from the rest of us. And it's in part of the fortress reserved for Otero and Dietrich, and the officers.''

Fenton grinned, but his eyes stayed small. ''I ain't allowed in that part of the place. Being only what you might call a common soldier.''

''Well, then . . .'' Clayburn said slowly, ''I guess I'll just have to become one of Dietrich's officers.''

Fenton shook his head. ''Ain't any officers in our outfit. Except Dietrich himself. Officially, he's supposed to be a Colonel under General Otero. Actually, he runs his own show. And the rest of us are just his men. No ranks.''

''Maybe we can change that. . . .'' Clayburn told Fenton exactly what he was to say to Dietrich in the morning, after Hogan left.

Fenton studied it—and Clayburn—carefully. ''It just *might* work,'' he admitted finally.

''Unless you've got a better idea . . . ?''

Fenton didn't. For some minutes they discussed the details. When they were finished, Fenton turned to leave.

''I'm really gonna enjoy myself tonight,'' he muttered, half to himself. ''Just in case I'm about to die on account of you, I sure don't want to go out feeling I've missed anything in life.''

When the door closed behind him, Clayburn crossed the room, uncorked the tequila bottle, and took a long swallow of the fiery stuff. Then another.

Serina drifted over beside him, watching him. ''I guess you need that,'' she said quietly. ''I do not blame you.''

''What I need,'' he told her, lowering the bottle, ''is one hell of a stretch of luck.''

Serina nodded, took the bottle from his hand, and drank

from it—not taking her eyes off him. She drank it down without a cough or a shudder.

Clayburn settled down on the straw pallet.

She put away the bottle, wiped her hand across her mouth, and asked evenly, "You are going to sleep again?"

"That's right."

She went to the other wall and took down his shirt. "This is dry now. You should wear it. It is damp in here." Her voice was low and even. Her thoughts seemed to be elsewhere.

Clayburn came up on one elbow. After a second he said, "All right."

Serina drifted over and knelt on his pallet, looking at him for a moment, holding the shirt in both hands. Her eyes looked down into his without expression.

"If we win," she said in the same low, even voice, "and you are still alive, perhaps you will not go away. If you stay, and are careful to work with the right persons, you could do very well for yourself here."

What she was up to was obvious. She was attempting to nudge him into helping her brother wind up on top in the power scramble.

He certainly didn't want to discourage her attempt. "You mean I could wind up—rich and respectable?"

One corner of her mouth quirked in a half smile. "All things are possible. . . ."

His own smile met hers. "Well—that's certainly something I'll have to think about."

She went on looking into his eyes. "Yes," she said softly. She put down the shirt and took his face between her slim hands and kissed him on the mouth.

It was a long, lingering kiss. When she finally released him something glowed darkly in the depths of his green eyes.

"That is for tomorrow," she whispered, ". . . for luck."

His hand closed on the back of her head. "I'm going to need more luck than that," he told her, and drew her down to him.

For an instant she tried to hold back, her dark eyes going wide at what was in his hard, sardonic face. But the hand cupping the back of her head was unyielding; his other hand closed on her waist. She came to him then, like a drawn bow.

ELEVEN

The sun had been up for three hours when Fenton and Clayburn turned their horses out of the village and followed the rutted dirt road toward the Losquadros Fortress. Hogan had gone out at dawn with the man named Seelig. Morales had not showed up—yet.

"I told Dietrich about you this morning," Fenton said as they rode, "just like you laid it out." He didn't look his old cheerful self this morning. His eyes were bloodshot and the soft flesh of his fat face sagged. "Told him I seen you once up in the Black Hills, so I knew who you were when I saw you in the cantina last night. You didn't know me, but I introduced myself and we got talking—and you got a little interested." Fenton's voice was more gravelly than it had been the night before, and uneven. "Dietrich bought it. I think."

"Stop being so damn nervous," Clayburn said through his teeth. "It shows."

"I'm *always* nervous." Fenton managed to get some of his usual grin in place. "What shows this morning is hangover. If you get to stick around long enough, you oughta try Dolores' place with me one night. Those girls of hers really know how to throw a party."

The high, thick stone walls of the fortress loomed ahead. They enclosed an area of about three acres. A lot of wall to defend. But Otero alone had enough troopers inside to do the job, even when Dietrich's bunch wasn't there. Clayburn looked at the cannons pointing down from the tops of the near wall's parapets. They looked like big eighteen-pounders; and there were enough of them to cover every approach to the front wall. There were riflemen on duty in the three sentry towers, and more at each of the embrasures spaced evenly between the cannon mounts.

Clayburn lowered his gaze from the top of the wall to the closed gateway ahead. The gate looked to be of solid oak, reinforced with heavy iron bands bolted on. It was big enough to admit a team of oxen pulling a high supply wagon. In one side of the main gate was cut a smaller door, just large enough to admit a single man or horse.

As they neared the gate, Fenton handed Clayburn a folded square of paper. "Your permission to enter."

Clayburn took it. "Will I need another of these to get out?"

Fenton nodded. "In or out, you need a permit. Signed and sealed by Dietrich himself."

They halted in front of the gate. Fenton waved a hand to the guards in the sentry tower above it. One of them turned away and called down to someone below. The door set in the main gate opened inward. Fenton swung to the ground and trudged through it, leading his horse. There was a tightening in Clayburn's guts as he dismounted and followed Fenton inside.

They entered a big open area that apparently served as the main parade grounds of the fortress. The armed guards stationed on either side of the gate eyed them blankly. The officer in charge of the guards took their permits, opened them, studied Dietrich's signature and the wax seal carefully. As he did so, Clayburn noted the four cannons behind a low earthen breastwork fifty yards away. Twelve-pounders, trained on the gate. Their artillery crews lounged behind them in the shade of an awning.

He noted, too, the ramps leading up from the parade grounds to the eighteen-pounders atop the walls. Each ramp heavily guarded. The whole place was solidly and professionally defended. Even a larger attacking force would play hell trying to batter its way in. And the cannons atop the walls were positioned so they could be swiftly turned around to fire down at any attackers who did manage to get inside.

The guard officer refolded the permits, tucked them away in his pocket, and nodded for them to move on. The door in the gate was shut and barred.

Clayburn looked around some more as he went with Fenton toward the corral and stables at one end of the parade grounds. The inner wall at the other end, and the entire length of the inner front wall, were lined with solid adobe buildings—barracks, blacksmith shed, bakery and kitchens, granary, harness shop, guardhouse; everything to be expected in a fort of this size.

What interested Clayburn more was the fourth side of the parade grounds. There the rest of the inside of the fortress was walled off behind a continual, unbroken line of high adobe buildings: powder magazine, arms storeroom, quartermaster's office and storehouse, hospital, commissary—and a few others he couldn't identify right off.

The center building, taller than the rest, had four sentries and two more twelve-pounders in front of it; and four riflemen standing guard duty on its flat roof. That would be the main headquarters.

Clayburn touched Fenton's arm and nodded at this inner row of buildings. "Officers' quarters on the other side of those?"

"Yeah. Regular troopers and the men in our outfit gotta stick to this side. And I ain't found a way to sneak through to the other side yet. I don't even know what that part of the place *looks* like."

They turned their horses over to a couple of Mexican troopers on duty at the company stables. Then Fenton turned and led the way back across the parade grounds toward the headquarters building.

"Well," he said tightly without moving his lips, "here goes. . . ."

They passed a sergeant putting a straggly bunch of troopers through their drill paces. Clayburn noticed that all the men going in and out of the buildings along the front wall were Mexican troopers—while none of the men lounging in the shade of the buildings against the end wall were.

"Dietrich's men and Otero's keep separate from each other?" he asked Fenton as they approached headquarters.

"Pretty much. We're a different breed. Leads to fights, sometimes. Had one in town last night, matter of fact. The Mex is dead. Our man ain't, but he's sure gonna be when Dietrich finishes with him."

The four guards in front of the center building were not Mexican. Fenton halted ten feet away from them. "Dietrich's expecting us," he announced. "Me and Captain Cullen."

One of the guards went inside. The other three looked Clayburn over. All three were of a type: hard, vicious, very sure of themselves. Gunfighters who lived past twenty had reason to be sure of themselves.

One of the three eyed Clayburn's soiled, trail-worn old clothes. *"Captain. . . ?"* He laughed and looked to Fenton. "Sure all that liquor you drank last night ain't done something to your head?"

Fenton smiled at him. A wide, cheerful smile that all of his fat face took part in. "I'll do something to *your* head, tonight, one more crack like that."

The other man met the steady stare of Fenton's little eyes— but not for long. He looked away and pretended boredom. But a nervous tick started in his right cheek as Fenton continued to smile at him.

The one who'd gone inside came out. "You can go in, Fenton." He looked at Clayburn. "You, too."

Clayburn followed Fenton inside, his long, lanky figure stiffly erect, his face impassive. They went past two more guards, down a short hot corridor, into a large office that was only a little less hot. Dietrich sat behind an impressive, beautifully carved oak desk, a strongly-built, blond man with piercing blue eyes in an arrogant, aristocratic face.

Fenton managed to look pleased with himself as he introduced Clayburn to Dietrich: "Here he is . . . Captain Cullen."

A Captain Cullen had been Chief of Scouts for General Wells in the campaign against the Apaches in Texas and New

Mexico. Clayburn had served as scout under him, briefly. And Fenton had said none of Dietrich's men had ever met Cullen—as far as he knew.

Dietrich's bright blue eyes examined Clayburn, measuring him. They were eyes that were used to taking a man's measure.

Finally Dietrich inclined his blond head slightly in greeting. "Captain. . . ."

Clayburn nodded politely. "Colonel. . . . A pleasure to make your acquaintance, Sir."

The military formality of his manner seemed to please Dietrich. He gestured at the chair beside his desk with a square, solidly-muscled hand. "Make yourself comfortable, Captain." He looked at Fenton. "You can leave."

Fenton turned and walked out without another look at Clayburn. But at least he didn't walk too fast.

Clayburn lowered himself into the chair. There was an armed gunfighter in each of the four corners of the room. They stood against the walls, looking at him blankly. If Dietrich took this kind of protection with him wherever he went, it was going to be a problem. Another problem, to add to the problem of getting out of this fortress. Clayburn had come down here to kill this man—but not to die with him.

After Fenton was gone, Dietrich turned back to Clayburn. "You don't mind my dismissing your friend?"

Clayburn looked at him coldly, "My *friend*?"

Dietrich smiled. "I beg your pardon, Captain. Of course a man like Fenton would not be considered a friend—by an officer and a gentleman."

Was his smile a little too amused? Before Clayburn could decide, the smile switched off. Dietrich glanced at his bodyguards. "But Fenton is typical of the sort of men under my command. Like these, here. What do you think of them . . . a scurvy lot?"

Clayburn shrugged carelessly. "All that matters about fighting men is whether they can fight. How well they fight depends entirely on leadership."

Again Dietrich seemed pleased. "Exactly." He leaned back in his chair. "I've heard about you, in the past, Captain

Cullen. You earned an excellent reputation for your work under General Wells. By the way, how *is* General Wells these days? I met him once, in Baltimore, a number of years back—along with that pretty wife of his.''

''He died last year—a bachelor.''

There was nothing in Dietrich's face to show that he had laid a trap which had caught nothing. ''Oh? Well perhaps the pretty woman I'm thinking of was some other officer's wife. I met so many of them. And to tell the truth, I was not particularly interested in who their husbands were.''

Clayburn smiled, just a little. His mind was very clear; his senses very alert, attuned to every faint change in Dietrich's voice and manner.

''Well now, Captain,'' Dietrich asked, ''what are you doing down here in Mexico?''

''I resigned my commission after General Wells died. His successor and I didn't get along. Put my savings into a mining venture, and lost every cent.'' This much fitted the real Captain Cullen, whom Clayburn had run into six months back in Montana. ''I'd heard there was a great deal of unrest down here. It seemed to me there might be a situation where my experience would be useful to someone. I intend to recoup my mining losses by selling that experience.''

''To me?''

''That depends,'' Clayburn said carefully. ''According to Fenton, you have no officers under your command.''

''That's true. But all of my men get officers' pay, nevertheless. Plus a generous share of any—ah—seizures, of enemy property.''

''Money is important to me,'' Clayburn told Dietrich. ''But so is my rank. I earned it. It's part of me. I won't serve in any command except as what I am. An officer.''

He leaned toward Dietrich, making his pitch. ''It seemed to me, Colonel, that you need a second-in-command. That's why I'm here. Surely there are routine operations where you'd prefer to send another out in command; times when you have more important things to do than lead your men in person. Certainly there are operations in which you have to split your command, and would prefer to have a competent, experienced officer in charge of the other half of your men."

It was a strong argument. A man with Captain Cullen's background would undoubtedly be an extremely valuable aid to Dietrich.

Dietrich became thoughtful. Clayburn gave him a moment, then prodded him mildly. "If I'm wrong, I'm wasting your time, Colonel. Because I won't settle for less."

The bright blue eyes continued to study Clayburn in silence.

Then Dietrich asked quietly: "Are you really Captain Cullen?"

Clayburn smiled. "You mean you doubt it?"

"I mean," Dietrich said, "that I would like to see your identity papers—commission, discharge, and so forth." His mouth was a thin, straight line. His eyes watched Clayburn coldly.

TWELVE

Clayburn's smile faded slowly. "Unfortunately, my papers were all lost in a mining camp fire. I wrote to Washington for copies, but that takes time as you know. They still hadn't arrived when I started south."

"That is unfortunate," Dietrich agreed.

Clayburn's face became stiff; his eyes as cold as Dietrich's. "It didn't occur to me that anyone would question my identity." He stood up. "It seems I *have* been wasting your time—and mine."

He started to turn away.

"Wait." Dietrich's voice was sharp.

Clayburn turned back and looked at him.

Dietrich's thin mouth softened. A little. "Sit down, Captain. I only meant that you look younger that I expected you to be, considering your reputation."

Clayburn began to smile again. "I'll take that as a compliment." He sat down, appearing to relax. "People usually do underestimate my age."

"It is the same with me," Dietrich said. "Perhaps this kind of life keeps some of us young. How old would you say I am?"

"I never judge a man's age. Only his ability."

Dietrich arched an elegant eyebrow. "*Touché*, Captain." He glanced toward the windows overlooking the parade grounds. "Well—what do you think of our fortifications?"

What he wanted to know, obviously, was whether Clayburn had made the kind of observations and judgments that a military officer of Captain Cullen's experience would make automatically.

Clayburn pursed his lips. "I haven't seen much of it."

"From what you have seen?"

"It seems to me the artillery on your walls could use more solid bracing. Of course they can be manually braced with tackle. But those eighteen-pounders have a tremendous recoil. With continual firing one of them could get out of hand and roll down the ramp."

"That's true," Dietrich conceded. "But I prefer to keep them mobile."

"So they can be turned on the parade grounds quickly, if necessary?"

"Exactly. . . . Anything else?"

Clayburn looked at the windows. "The position of the four twelve-pounders commanding the gate seemed a bit weak to me."

"Weak?"

Clayburn nodded. "They're loaded with grape and chainshot, I imagine?"

"Yes."

"Well, that'll stop a massed charge, of course. But suppose the gate is caved in and the enemy tries slipping through one or two at a time? You'd get only a few men with each gun. Four shots—and before they can be reloaded the rest of the enemy would be on them."

"We have riflemen inside. Excellent marksmen."

"The best marksmen can miss in the dark. With a lot of fast-moving targets."

Dietrich eyed him approvingly. "What would you suggest?"

"A stockade, fanning out from the guns to the wall on both sides of the gate. That way, anyone breaking it will be slowed up, penned in long enough for your riflemen to hit them. Long enough for the cannons to reload."

"You have excellent eye for such things. I have been giving that some thought myself lately." Dietrich turned from the windows. "With your background, you would be an excellent tracker, of course. That, too, would be of great value."

"I've never met the man who was better at it," Clayburn told him, factually.

"Oh? I have a very good tracker. His name's Hogan. I'd like to test you against him sometime—just for the sport of it, naturally."

Clayburn grinned. "Sounds interesting. Where do I find this man?"

But Dietrich was not a man to be loose with information. "He's off on a mission for me, at the moment," he said. And that was all he had to say, on that subject. He eyed Clayburn a moment longer and then appeared to make up his mind. "As for whether your abilities in actual battle equal your reputation—that, of course, will have to wait until we go into the field to be proved."

"Does that mean I've got the job as your second-in-command?"—

"It means we'll see when the time comes. When I've had a chance to observe you in action. Meanwhile, consider yourself my guest."

Clayburn frowned a little. "Your guest?"

Dietrich nodded. "With full officer's privileges, of course. I think you'll find our officers' quarters quite comfortable. And if you should turn out to be all that I've heard, your pay will begin as of now. Is that fair?"

"Fair enough," Clayburn agreed.

Dietrich stood up. The Colt on his hip was holstered low, with a thong around his thigh securing it in place. "Now I have something to attend to." He looked at one of his bodyguards. "Have Anderson brought from the guard house."

As the bodyguard went out, Dietrich turned back to Clayburn. "One of my men killed one of General Otero's troopers last night in a town brawl. He strangled him to death. I don't allow any of the men to carry weapons when they're not on duty. Fighting is to be expected, in any army. But killing among us. . . . What would you say his punishment should be?"

Clayburn shrugged. "It's a capital offense—in any army."

"Precisely." Dietrich came around his desk and started for the door, motioning to Clayburn. "Come. . . ."

Clayburn followed him out of the building. The body-guards followed Clayburn, and spread out behind Dietrich when they were outside.

Anderson, the killer, was being marched across the sun-baked parade grounds from the guard house, by two men holding his arms. He was a scrawny, scar-faced man. As soon as they stopped in front of Dietrich, he began to babble: "Listen to me, Colonel—please. I didn't mean to do it. . . . I was drunk. . . . We were both drunk. And anyway he started it. He . . ."

Anderson fell silent before Dietrich's expressionless stare. All over the parade grounds, the men had stopped what they were doing to watch. Some were grinning. Fenton was among them; but not grinning. Dietrich motioned to the men holding the prisoner, and they let him go, stepping back. Anderson immediately folded his arms across his chest as though hugging himself for some feeling of protection.

He cowered before Dietrich's continued stare. "If you'll just listen to how it was!" he pleaded. "I mean he got me mad, and I lost my head and. . . ."

Dietrich pointed a finger to the other end of the parade grounds. "If you can make it to that wall, I won't have you executed for what you did."

Anderson gaped at him. "What . . . ? I don't. . . ."

"It's your only chance," Dietrich told him tonelessly. "You'd better try. . . . *Now!*"

Anderson fell back a step, looked uncertainly from Dietrich to the other end of the parade grounds. Then, suddenly, he was running, as fast as he could. Racing toward that distant wall.

Dietrich grabbed a carbine from one of the sentries. "Captain, I've heard you're a crack shot." He threw it at Clayburn. "Stop him."

Clayburn caught the thrown carbine, levering as he brought it up, firing with the instant of taking snap-aim.

Anderson toppled to the ground with a howl. Rolled in the dust and sat up—and stopped yelling as he realized that he was not hurt. Clayburn had shot away one of his bootheels.

Dietrich looked at Clayburn. "That," he said slowly, "was

superb shooting, Captain. . . . But when I ordered you to stop him I meant. . . . ''

"I know what you meant," Clayburn told him coolly. "I'm only your guest for the moment, remember? Until you confirm my position in your command your orders don't apply to me."

He smiled at Dietrich. It was going to be an intense pleasure, killing this man.

Dietrich smiled back at him, thinly. "Squeamish?"

Clayburn shrugged a shoulder. "He wasn't under *my* command when he committed the murder, Colonel. He was under yours."

And he threw the carbine back at Dietrich.

Dietrich whirled and levered as it hit his hands. He fired twice in rapid succession. Anderson screamed and clapped his hands to his ears. Dietrich has shot off both his earlobes.

Clayburn looked from Anderson to Dietrich. "You're a pretty fair shot yourself, Colonel. But what's the point of all this? Why not just execute him and be done with it?"

"This *does* bother you."

Clayburn looked bored. "It's a waste of time."

Dietrich laughed, and looked at the men who'd brought Anderson across the parade grounds. "Take him back to the guard house and stick his head in a bucket of water until he drowns."

The two men started off toward Anderson. Dietrich turned back to Clayburn. "That is the punishment for such small offenses under my command. For larger crimes—such as failure to perform properly in action, or betrayal—the execution is much more painful; and much slower. Be sure to remember that."

"I'll remember it," Clayburn said evenly.

"Good. Come. . . . I'll introduce you to one of Otero's officers who'll find you quarters."

Clayburn went back into the building with Dietrich. The four bodyguards followed them in, keeping a respectful distance but staying within close gun range. Out on the parade grounds Anderson began to cry for mercy.

THIRTEEN

The officer who took Clayburn to his new quarters was Lieutenant Decolta, and he was in charge of the guard system in the other part of the fortress—the section that Fenton hadn't been able to get into. Which made Decolta a man whom Clayburn wanted to get to know a lot better.

Lieutenant Decolta was slim, with a narrow handsome face and a thin dark mustache. He was a vain man. The vanity was betrayed by the careful combing of his sleek, thinning hair to cover the places where he was going bald. It was evident, too, in the polished gleam of his boots, the tailoring of his neatly-pressed uniform and the shine of its gold braid. Being on duty, he wore a dress sword in addition to the pistol in his silver decorated holster.

Clayburn followed Decolta through a corridor in the rear of Dietrich's headquarters building, out across an open passage, and under a wide archway opening into a maze of passageways and stone and adobe-brick buildings. This part of the fortress was older, its open spaces surfaced with worn cobblestones. Armed soldiers on sentry duty saluted as they passed; Decolta didn't bother to acknowledge them.

"Here is the officers' quarters," Decolta said as he led the way across a small, open square toward a two-story stone building that merged into other buildings.

"This where Dietrich and General Otero live?" Clayburn asked as they approached it.

"Oh, no." Decolta pointed to a high-towered stone building adjacent to it. "The General and Colonel Dietrich occupy that one.'' Pointing to an adobe-brick building on the other side of the square, he went on, ''The officers' dining room is in there. The building next to it is for those whose wives are with them.''

''That's where you're quartered?''

Decolta shook his head. ''My family is in San Filipe.'' He didn't sound unhappy about it.

They entered a small doorway in the single officer's building, went up a narrow corkscrew flight of brick steps to the second floor and down a hall. Decolta opened a door and motioned Clayburn in with a courtly gesture.

The room was small but clean, with a single window and heavy furniture. There was a large, comfortable-looking bed, a bureau with a washbasin on it and a gilt-framed mirror over it; several solid, leather-padded chairs and a table; a teak closet and a large chest. There was even a round carpet in the middle of the stone floor.

''Satisfactory?'' Decolta asked from the doorway.

''Fine—by the way, what do we do for amusement here?''

''Amusement? . . . Well, when one is off duty there is a good deal of gambling, of course.'' He arched an eyebrow at Clayburn. ''Ah . . . do you like the cards, Captain?''

Clayburn recognized the tone. Lieutenant Decolta was vain about his gambling prowess, too. ''I play—when there's nothing else to do and the stakes are high enough to add some spice.''

''So? . . . Perhaps we will play, you and I, when I am off duty.''

''I'd enjoy it. But I was thinking of other amusements. . . .'' Clayburn glanced across the room to the bed. ''Something like that should be shared.'' He smiled at the lieutenant. ''Surely a man like you—with your wife so far away. . . .''

Lieutenant Decolta relished the implied compliment to his virility. ''Of course. . . . But not here. The women are all in the town. There is one magnificent place. . . .''

''Yes, Fenton told me. Dolores' house?''

Decolta made a face. ''That is for the enlisted men. And for common swine like Fenton. For officers—for men such as you and I, Captain—there is another place. With the most exquisite ladies, I assure you. Some there by choice; others that we have—ah, *persuaded* to return with us from our various campaigns. Those I like best. Perhaps you would care to accompany me some night?''

"Perhaps. Where are your quarters, Lieutenant? In case I get bored and want company."

Lieutenant Decolta shook his head regretfully. ''My room is in another part of the building. General Otero, Colonel Dietrich and myself are the only officers allowed in there.''

Which made Decolta even more interesting for Clayburn.

Decolta turned to leave. ''I must make the rounds of my sentry posts now, Captain. I will see you at dinner this evening.''

''I'll look forward to it.''

Decolta went off along the hall, in the opposite direction from which they'd come. Clayburn went to the doorway and watched him go. At the other end of the hall was a heavy oak door. Decolta took a ring of keys from his pocket and unlocked the door. He went through, closing the door behind him. Clayburn could hear him re-locking it from the other side.

Yes, without a doubt, Lieutenant Decolta would be the one to concentrate on.

Clayburn crossed his room and looked out the window. Below was a small cobbled courtyard, enclosed on three sides by the rear walls of stone buildings. On the fourth side was a portion of the high rear wall of the fortress. There were three sentries in sight atop this portion of the wall. And low down in the inner face of the wall was a closed door.

Only one of the buildings had a door to the courtyard, as far as Clayburn could see. But there was a projection in the outside wall just below his window, which prevented him from seeing whether there were any windows or doors in the lower portion of the building containing his own room, facing out on the courtyard.

The door that he could see was in a building across the courtyard from him. It was shut, and it was made of heavy timbers with thick bands of iron cross-bolted to them. And there were no windows in that building. Two sentries stood guard before this door, each holding a new Winchester and wearing a saber. Also guarding this door was a single twelve-pounder cannon with a three-man gun crew.

Clayburn studied the building intently. It was only one story high, its walls of solid stone. And that business of no windows at all. . . .

He was looking, Clayburn knew, at the building containing Otero's loot.

Lieutenant Decolta appeared atop the rear wall of the fortress, coming up out of the wall itself. Which meant there was a passageway of some kind in the interior of the wall. Decolta inspected the three entries on the wall there, turned about, and vanished down into the interior of the wall again.

Ten seconds later the door in the bottom of the inner face of the fortress wall opened, and Decolta stepped out into the courtyard. Through the opened door, Clayburn made out a dim inner passageway. There'd be a flight of steps leading up from it to the top of the wall. Clayburn pursed his lips thoughtfully.

The sentries and gun crew in front of the treasure-house door came stiffly to attention. Decolta looked them over, pushed at the door behind them—a routine check to make sure it was locked. It was. Clayburn was willing to lay odds that this was one door for which Lieutenant Decolta did not have a key.

Decolta re-crossed the courtyard and disappeared into the rear wall of the fortress, shutting the door behind him. And locking it from inside? Clayburn gazed at the fortress wall, his eyes gradually rising to its ramparts. Some two hundred yards beyond, the red cliff of the back of the canyon rose sheer toward the sky.

In the silence, Clayburn could hear the sound of water: the river, rushing past the length of the rear wall of the fortress, forming a deep, naturally swift-flowing moat. No attacking force could get across that river to the wall, so fast was the current at that point. Any attempt to bridge the river or get across with rope-secured rafts would be so slow that all the attackers would be picked off by the rifles and cannon atop the wall before they got across.

Beyond the rear of the fortress, the river rushed on and plunged into the hole in the base of the cliff. Legend had it that long ago a man had fallen into the river and been carried through that hole. One day later he had emerged from the other side of the mountains, where the river reappeared, flowing out into a valley.

That was legend. What was not legend was that in recent times three other men had gone through that hole into the depths under the mountains. One had fallen in; another had dived in on a dare; the third had been thrown in. Two had never been seen again. The third emerged a week later from the other side of the mountains, completely mad, unable to describe anything about his ordeal except to babble about the interminable darkness he'd wandered through.

Legend had it that the river flowed through "The Belly of Hell." This was the escape route Clayburn and the others intended to use. Because it was the only escape route possible. And they'd be taking along one thing that the others who'd gone into the depths under the mountains hadn't: light.

Clayburn continued to watch through the window. The minutes went by. Then nine soldiers came marching into sight from directly below him. Two of them took over guard duty in front of the door of the windowless building across the courtyard. Three others replaced the gun crew there. The remaining four entered the door in the fortress wall. Three of them appeared moments later atop the wall. The sentries they replaced there vanished down inside the wall. They came out through the door in its base; with one other—which meant there was a guard *inside* the wall. All nine men going off duty left the courtyard by marching across toward Clayburn and disappearing below him. Which meant there was some kind of doorway in the ground floor.

But though Clayburn leaned out the window, trying to see what was below the wall projection under it, he could not see anything of the lower portion of this side of the building. And it was essential that he find out what was there.

He turned and left his room, going down the winding steps. He could find no way to the courtyard. And there was no door or corridor by which he could enter the lower floor of the officers' building.

For a time Clayburn studied the adjacent building, the one serving as living quarters for Otero and Dietrich. There were troopers on guard in its entrance, and more to be seen through the windows. If he was calculating correctly, the rear of that building also was on the inner courtyard, across from the treasure house. But there was no way by daylight to check on this.

Clayburn strolled away from the officers' building and worked his way back toward the other section of the fortress— the part that surrounded the main parade grounds. He took his time about it, wandering in and out of passageways, looking for another route than the one Decolta had used bringing him in here. If anyone spotted him at it and questioned him, he intended to pass it off by explaining he'd gotten lost.

But he didn't find another way through. None of the buildings flanking Dietrich's headquarters had doors on this side— except one: the armory room, down at the far end. And this door was shut, with a sentry on guard in front of it. When Clayburn approached, the sentry demanded his permit to enter. Clayburn shook his head, smiled, and wandered away.

Finally he went through the way he'd come—entering the rear of the headquarters building. Since all the guards there, inside and out, had seen him with Dietrich and Decolta, they let him pass without question. There were one hell of a lot of them, guarding every corridor and doorway.

He ran into Dietrich as he neared the front entrance. Dietrich smiled his frosty smile, and asked how he liked his room.

"It'll do," Clayburn told him. "I'm going to take my saddlebags in now." He didn't mention his weapons. That was something he was saving for when the time was ripe.

"After you do, come to my office," Dietrich told him. "I'll bring you up to date on the situation we have here."

Dietrich continued on his way. Clayburn went to the front doorway and stood there in its shadow for a few moments, scanning all the men in sight around the parade grounds. If Morales had returned, he was not anywhere in sight. But that was what kept the tension twisted tight inside Clayburn:

Morales and the time element. The longer it took to get the job done, the more time it gave in which Morales might return and spot him. And this was a job that was going to take time to work out.

Clayburn went down the parade grounds to the corral and stables. As he'd expected, Fenton was there waiting for him, leaning against a wall and smoking nervously.

He dropped his cigarette and ground it under his heel as soon as Clayburn appeared. "Did you locate it?" he whispered.

Clayburn nodded. "I'll see you tonight, in town," he said shortly. One of the soldiers on stable duty was coming in their direction. Clayburn moved on, got his saddlebags, and headed back across the parade grounds.

After leaving his things in his room, he spent the rest of that morning and early afternoon with Dietrich in his office. There was a large wall map of the area Otero claimed for his own. Dietrich went over this map with Clayburn, in detail; filling him in on the situation, showing him where they'd almost cornered the main rebel band a few days ago, where they'd lost them, and the approximate area Dietrich suspected the rebels were now hiding in.

"I don't think they'll try any major action against us," Dietrich said, "until Juan Ramirez returns. A rumor has reached us that an outlaw named Latigo has joined Ramirez, and has become his second-in-command. But Ramirez remains their real leader. Many of the rebels are from proud families. They would not accept the leadership of a man like Latigo in anything important."

Knowing Latigo's ambitions, Clayburn wondered how many of those men of proud families the outlaw figured on killing, later, in order to wind up the important man Serina expected her brother to become. "Where is this Ramirez?" he asked Dietrich.

"We are not sure. He went north of the border. One of my men found him—then lost him. But another of my men heard something up there about Ramirez. I have sent them both back to check on it."

"Back where?"

"North," Dietrich said, and changed the subject. Turning to the map, he pointed out a town marked on it. "This is a small village. But there is a rumor some of its men have joined the rebels, and that they have arms hidden there. One of my spies has gone there to investigate. He will be back in a few days. If the rumor is true, I will send about fifteen of my men there—to execute every single person in that village."

He looked at Clayburn. "Perhaps this would be a perfect operation to try you out on. Would you care to lead it, and carry out the executions?"

Clayburn eyed the map unemotionally. "It sounds fairly routine. Should be able to handle it easy enough, with fifteen men."

"Unless the rebels ambush you with a larger force."

Clayburn smiled thinly. "I don't think so. A lot of very smart Apaches have tried ambushing me. Without success."

"So? . . . Well, we'll see."

A few days—that didn't leave much time, even if Morales didn't show up.

Dietrich took out a gold watch and looked at it. "Would you join me for lunch?"

They ate in a small, private dining room in the building Dietrich shared with Otero. It was an excellent meal, except for the presence of the four armed bodyguards. Those gunmen followed Dietrich everywhere, never letting him out of their sight—or anyone who was near Dietrich.

Between them, and all the other armed men all over this fortress, Clayburn began to accept the fact that there was only one way to kill Dietrich—and survive. That was Juan's way: arming a force large enough to smash the army that surrounded Dietrich. But arming a force that large would take money—and there was only one way to get the money.

So unless Dietrich happened to get within range when the time came to break out of here. . . .

Nothing in Clayburn's manner betrayed these thoughts as he politely discussed war with Dietrich, who professed an interest in Captain Cullen's experiences in various military actions he'd heard about. Clayburn had been part of enough campaigns and battles with Captain Cullen to describe several in satisfactory detail.

Dietrich went on to a theoretical discussion of a number of history's more interesting battles. The books Clayburn had read on military strategy during his stint as scout for the army helped him to keep up his end of the conversation. They were re-fighting Napoleon's retreat from Moscow when General Otero put in an appearance.

He was a short, compact man in his early fifties, with bleak dark eyes in a sour face. His mouth looked like a locked purse, and there was a lot of nervous energy in the way he moved and held himself. His uniform was not as well pressed as Lieutenant Decolta's, and his gold braid needed shining; if he was vain, it wasn't about things that showed.

Clayburn noted that only two bodyguards followed Otero into the room, as compared to Dietrich's four. He noted, too, that Dietrich did not bother to rise as he made the introductions:

"General Otero . . . Captain Cullen, the new officer I was telling you about."

Clayburn stood up and said something polite.

Otero said nothing. He looked Clayburn over with apparent disinterest, and then gave his attention to Dietrich. "Why are no preparations being made to go out after the rebels again?" he snapped.

Dietrich took a sip of brandy before replying. "All in good time, General." His manner with Otero was casual, almost, but not quite, to the point of insolence. "Care to join us? This veal is delicious."

Otero's tight mouth twitched with irritation. "I have already eaten. There is nothing else to do while we have to remain here and wait for the country around us to become safe to travel through. When I gave you this job, you assured me that you would soon wipe out all the rebels."

"And I will," Dietrich told him, unperturbed. "Soon."

"Soon! You continue to say soon—while I wait. And wait."

Dietrich smiled at Otero. "It can only be accomplished by moving slowly, and carefully. Of course, if you feel I'm not doing well enough to suit you, General—you can always go out there and hunt them down yourself.''

Otero's bleak dark eyes narrowed. He turned away without another word, and left the room with the two bodyguards trailing him. Dietrich's four bodyguards watched them go, then returned their attention to Clayburn and the various doorways and windows.

Dietrich took another sip of brandy, as though to rid his mouth of a bad aftertaste of Otero's sourness. "That," he sneered, "is our General Otero for you."

"Is he always that angry?"

Dietrich laughed. "He is not actually a military man like us. Only a politician. Politicians know nothing."

"They usually wind up running everything," Clayburn remarked mildly, "after the military men have finished with their fighting."

Dietrich's hand closed into a fist around his brandy glass. "Not this time," he said softly—and let it go at that.

After the meal, Dietrich returned to his office with his bodyguards. Clayburn went to his room and stood at the window, gazing down on the low, windowless, guarded building on the other side of the small courtyard. He'd been there only a few minutes when there was a knock at his door.

He crossed to the door and opened it. Otero stood there, his two bodyguards in the hall behind him. The tight mouth actually smiled. "Captain Cullen, are your quarters comfortable?''

"Very. . . . Care to come in, General?"

Otero stepped in. He shut the door behind him, leaving the two bodyguards outside. "I neglected to welcome you here when we were introduced, Captain. Forgive me."

"That's all right."

"I was upset, with Colonel Dietrich," Otero said carefully, watching Clayburn's face as he said it.

There was nothing to be read in Clayburn's face. "I could see that, General."

"It is only that I sometimes have the feeling that Dietrich forgets *I* am the general here. Ah, well—from what Dietrich has told me, you will be of great use to me . . . to us. A man of your background will be able to take many of Dietrich's duties off his hands.''

Clayburn nodded. ''That was my thought.''

''Perhaps in an emergency,'' Otero went on, ''you would even be able to take over *all* his duties.'' He spoke carefully, but his eyes were not careless.

''That would depend on the emergency.''

''Of course, Captain. Yes, I am sure you are going to be most valuable to me. I do not only mean in wiping out the rebels. Also afterward. You could do very well for yourself, here. With me.''

It was almost exactly what Serina had said, as part of her attempt to get him behind her brother.

''I understand, General,'' Clayburn said. And he did. Dietrich was planning to double-cross Otero and take over. And Otero, not at all unaware of this, was getting himself some insurance against such a double cross.

''I was sure you would,'' Otero said, without expression. ''Goodbye now, Captain. Feel free to come see me—any time there is anything you care to discuss.''

The tight mouth worked up another brief smile, and Otero was gone. Clayburn stared at the door for some time before going back to his observation post at the window.

Clayburn ate dinner that night in the officers' dining room. Lieutenant Decolta introduced him to the other officers present, but Clayburn was only interested in Decolta. Decolta, flattered at having all of the new Captain's attention focused on himself, sat together with Clayburn at the table. After the meal, the two of them settled down together in Clayburn's quarters to play cards.

Lieutenant Decolta was a skilled gambler. But his skill was flawed by his vanity, which extended to a reckless belief in his own luck. He took long, unwarranted chances. Clayburn won steadily for the first hour, which Decolta didn't like at all. Then Clayburn let him win back all he'd lost, which the lieutenant liked very much indeed.

After that Clayburn let Decolta win a little extra from him, and called it quits: "I thought I had you there, for awhile. But it looks like my luck has run out."

Lieutenant Decolta grinned. "I can usually depend on Lady Luck to come to my rescue. And speaking of ladies— I feel in the mood for some of the ones I mentioned to you. Want to come with me?"

"Not tonight. I'm still tired from all that riding the past week, getting here. Maybe tomorrow night."

"Well, in case you change your mind later. . . ." Decolta told him how to find the place he was going to in the town.

After Lieutenant Decolta left, Clayburn waited about an hour. Then he went to the stables, saddled his horse. At the gate, he gave the officer of the guard his permit to leave, and picked up the one he'd need to get back in. Dietrich had explained the arrangement when he'd given Clayburn the permit to leave, earlier in the day. Now that Clayburn was part of the fortress garrison, there would always be the two permits—to leave and enter—waiting for him with the guard at the gate.

It was an arrangement that Clayburn had already made part of the plan he was beginning to work out.

Riding away from the fortress, he followed the night-shadowed road toward the town. There were clouds in the night sky, hiding the moon. He was more than halfway to the town, turning a bend in the road past a field of tall corn, when a horse and rider appeared out of the darkness just ahead of him; coming around the bend toward the fortress.

Clayburn kept his sorrel to the same steady, slow pace as they rode toward each other. The stock of a rifle poked up from the saddle scabbard of the other horse, and the faint starlight glinted on the ivory grip of a gun holstered on its rider's hip. Which meant he was one of Dietrich's men just arriving, with a permit that entitled him to remain armed all the way to the fortress.

The other man's form was big and bulky in the night. His face was shadowed by his hatbrim, as was Clayburn's. It was not until the distance between them was almost closed that they recognized each other.

It was Morales.

FOURTEEN

Clayburn twisted the reins and kicked his horse savagely, ramming it full-tilt into the other horse before Morales could react. As the other horse rocked back from the impact, Morales grabbed for the gun in his holster. Clayburn flung himself out of his saddle and slammed into Morales' shoulder first, tearing him from his horse and carrying him to the ground with him.

They landed hard, with Clayburn on top. The gun bounced out of Morales' fingers and skittered away in the darkness. Clayburn's knees rammed into Morales' middle, knocking the wind out of him and stopping him from yelling. A shout probably wouldn't carry to the fortress from here, and the town would be pretty noisy by this time of night. But anyone who happened to be traveling the road might be near enough to hear, and come to investigate. So Clayburn's next move, a split-second after they hit the ground, was to attempt to club his forearm across the other man's throat.

Morales blocked it with his shoulder, twisted, and slammed one of those sledgehammer fists to the side of Clayburn's jaw. It knocked him off, rolling him in the dust. Morales came up on one knee. Clayburn's right leg jerked up and out, smashing his bootheel against Morales' face, It broke the tip of the man's nose and caved in his front teeth. Morales cried out as he fell back. But the cry was stifled when he began choking on his own blood, and didn't carry more than ten yards away.

They scrambled to their feet at the same time. Clayburn

launched himself at the bigger man, slamming a left and right into his midsection. It was like hitting a full-grown oak. The thick layers of muscle hardly gave at all. Morales grunted, fell back a step, and spat out blood and snapped-off tooth splinters. Then his left fist was pistoning out, ramming into Clayburn's chest and staggering him backward.

Morales came after him. Clayburn set himself and drove the heel of his hand up against the broken, bleeding nose. Morales took it and grappled for Clayburn, his left hand clamping the back of his neck, the thumb of his other hand stabbing for Clayburn's eye. Clayburn jerked up his head and caught the thumb between his teeth, bit down on it hard at the same time that his knee jerked up into Morales' groin.

Morales yelled and yanked himself away, bending over to ease his agony. His yell had been louder than the last one. Clayburn had to do something about that. He was faster than his hulking enemy, and ordinarily he could have kept away from those huge, swinging fists and taken his time about slicing Morales up. But in this case he had to stop his yelling. And there was only one way it could be done in a hurry; a way that meant he'd have to take everything Morales could throw at him.

His face was a sullen, stubborn mask as he closed with Morales, taking a roundhouse slam to the head and another against his jaw. His vision fogged and dizziness swirled in his brain. But within the dizziness a small core remained deadly clear. Morales tried to knee him. He deflected the knee with his hip, and twisted with it, shoving in closer, all of him a single unit of concentrated, flowing power. He blocked a punch with his left arm and clubbed Morales across the nose with his right fist. Once . . . twice . . . Morales slammed a left into his stomach. Clayburn took it, and hit that ruined nose two more times with everything he had behind the clubbing fist.

With his nose smashed flat, Morales could no longer breath through it. He had to breath now through his wide-open mouth. And he couldn't breathe through it, swallow blood, and yell very loud all at the same time. But he was far from finished. All of his face from the nose down streamed blood; but his eyes blazed with pure, unadulterated hate. He slammed another fist into Clayburn's middle that buckled his knees; then tried to break his ankle with a kick.

Clayburn sidestepped and backed away, breathing hard through his bared teeth, trying to gain enough time for the dizziness to ebb. Morales lunged after him. Clayburn dodged a slashing fist, blocked a kick with his knee, kept backing away. His chest was heaving and his arms hung at his sides. The haze began to leave his eyes.

Morales charged. This time Clayburn did not dodge. He ducked under a roundhouse swing and brought his right fist up from his knees, slamming it off the bottom of Morales' chin. Morales stopped dead in his tracks, swaying. Clayburn bent forward and hit Morales three times in the stomach, leaning all his strength into each murderous, chopping blow. The muscle barrier across the big man's middle finally gave way under the pile-driving force of Clayburn's fists. He made a gagging, straining sound deep inside him. Clayburn hit him again, in exactly the same place. Morales began backing away.

Clayburn followed. A huge fist came out of nowhere and exploded against the side of his head, stopping him momentarily. He shook his head hard, to clear it. And then he was closing in again, remembering the beating Morales had given him when his hands had been tied behind his back, and two men had been holding him. . . .

He hit Morales in the jaw, twisting his shoulders behind it, feeling his knuckles flatten as the impact rocked the other man's head. His left fist caught Morales betwen the eyes, stunning him. His right hammered into Morales' mouth, breaking more teeth, driving him backward gasping and gulping for air. Clayburn stayed with him like an efficient, single-purpose engine of destruction. He paid the price for it, taking desperate, bone-jarring punches as he bored in. But Morales had been sapped of half his strength, and his fists lashed out wildly, landing by chance. Clayburn paid him back with measured, unerring blows that thudded into the stomach, whipped the ruined face, shifted back to the mid-section.

Morales suddenly stumbled and sagged forward, his fore-head falling against Clayburn's chest, his hands clutching. Before Clayburn could shake him off, Morales straightened up with a jerk, the hard top of his skull ramming the under-side of Clayburn's chin.

Clayburn was flung backwards, staggering to keep from going down. He managed to catch his balance and come to a halt still standing. But he was swaying dizzily, his head wobbling, arms hanging limp. Morales scented his last chance for a kill. Gathering all the reserve he had left, he lunged forward.

Clayburn's dazed appearance abruptly disappeared. He sidestepped the charge. Morales lurched past, and Clayburn twisted around behind him. Before Morales could recover, Clayburn's left hand was against the back of his head and Clayburn's left elbow was digging into the back of his shoulder. Clayburn's right forearm had slid across the front of Morales' throat and his right hand locked around his left wrist. Morales struggled to throw him off. But Clayburn's knee came up into the small of Morales' back, shoving him forward while the terrible strangling forearm across his throat continued to pull him backward.

Morales threw himself backward to the ground, landing on top of Clayburn in an attempt to dislodge him. Clayburn hung on, steadily increasing the pressure across the thick throat. Morales fought to get air into his lungs, and could not. The blood trapped in his head was pounding against the inside of his skull as he struggled up on his knees, with Clayburn still attached to him, the forearm like an iron bar digging deep into the throat.

Morales fell face down with Clayburn on top of him. Clay-burn hung on, maintaining the terrible pressure of the stran-glehold. Morales' struggles became feeble, aimless—and finally ceased. Still Clayburn did not let go.

He did not let go until Morales was the way he wanted him: dead.

An hour later Clayburn rode into the town, leading Morales' horse. The dirt streets were crowded with Otero's troopers and Dietrich's men. But they were all too preoccupied with their drunken roistering to pay him any attention. Avoiding the plaza where most of the ones outside were concentrated, he reached the stable and turned both horses over to Roa. He had found Morales' hand gun, and he took that with him into the connecting building, rolled in the gunbelt. In his other hand he carried Morales' rifle.

Going down the steps at the end of the corridor, Clayburn rapped at the low door with the rifle muzzle. Serina opened the door, and blinked when she saw what he looked like. He had washed his face and hands at the river, and used the cold water to soak the bloodstains from his clothing as much as possible. But there was no concealing the livid bruises, his cut cheek, or the dark swelling along his jaw.

He stepped into the small cellar room. Joe Fenton was there. So was Latigo, wearing the ragged clothes of a poor farmer or shepherd. They stared at him the way Serina had. Clayburn shut the door behind him and told them what had happened. He made it short and to the point.

"I buried Morales under the soft dirt in the river bank. He isn't likely to be found until the water washes that dirt away."

Fenton was scowling. "When Dietrich finds out Morales came in—and never reached the fortress—he's gonna. . . ."

"He won't find out," Clayburn said, "until the officer who passed Morales through the canyon entrance hears somebody wondering when Morales is going to show up."

"Something," Latigo pointed out quietly, "which can occur at any time after that officer goes off duty."

Clayburn nodded. "We'll have to do it sooner than we expected. Tomorrow night." He put the rifle and gunbelt on a packing case, and told them what he had worked out so far.

Latigo listened carefully, his handsome face clenched, eyes narrow. "Tomorrow night. . . ." he murmured softly when Clayburn had finished. "But can you do what has to be done by then?"

"I'll have to."

Latigo turned to his sister. "Serina, Gila is waiting with the horses in the outer canyon. As soon as it is light tomorrow morning, you will leave and go to him. Start at once for the other side of the mountains. By moving quickly you will be there before us. Wait until we emerge . . ." A faint smile touched the corners of Latigo's reckless mouth. ". . . *if* we emerge."

Serina nodded without looking away from Clayburn. She hadn't said a word or taken her eyes off him since he'd entered.

Latigo turned back to Clayburn. "We will have to move very swiftly tomorrow night. You must know every step of the way by then; and each thing we will have to deal with. Any moment we waste searching the way, any hesitation, may be fatal." His words were spoken grimly, but there was a feverish anticipation in his eyes.

Fenton was different. His anticipation was tempered by a sensible nervousness. "It's gonna be goddamn chancey, with just the three of us. I been prayin' Ramirez would show up with a couple more to help."

"I'd guess he's on his way by now," Clayburn said. "Maybe he'll make it on time."

Latigo doubted it. "That doctor in Tubavi Springs said Juan Ramirez would not be able to ride for a week. . . ."

"The doctor didn't know much about Juan," Clayburn told him. "I remember one time Juan had a horse he was breaking fall on him. That time a doctor said he wouldn't be able to ride again for a month. He was riding in a week."

"Well if he *is* coming," Fenton said, "he's only got one more day to get here. If he doesn't. . . ."

"If he does not," Latigo completed it for him, "we will do it ourselves. The three of us."

They discussed the details for some time, going over each one carefully. After they were done, Clayburn left the room and climbed the steps into the narrow corridor leading to the stable. Behind him, the cellar door at the bottom of the steps opened and closed again. Turning, he saw Serina coming up after him.

"Your face. . . ." she said softly when she reached him. "Dietrich will see—and wonder what happened. What will you tell him?"

"Enough of the truth to get by."

Her hand came up and touched gently at the swelling along his jaw. "Does it hurt very much?"

"It hurts," he said flatly. She had moved closer, her soft, supple figure touching him, stirring a memory of her wild hunger with him through the previous night. He smiled thinly. "Your brother send you up here to do some more persuading?"

"No." The corners of her mouth quirked. "And do not think you trick me. I have known too many men to be made a fool of. I know you would not become disloyal to your friend Juan Ramirez, for any reason."

Clayburn stared at her. "And last night . . . did you know then?"

"I knew. . . ." Her body pressed tightly against him as her arms slid around his neck. "For luck. . . ." she whispered, and kissed his bruised mouth. "I'm sorry that this night I cannot give you more luck."

She turned quickly and went back down to the cellar room. Clayburn stood there for a moment, gazing after her. Then he moved away through the corridor into the stable. There was much to be done while the darkness lasted. It was going to be a dangerous night.

FIFTEEN

It was past midnight when Lieutenant Decolta emerged from the big hacienda with the high, vine-covered walls on the edge of town. He was unsteady on his feet as he walked to the hitchrack for his horse. And he had some difficulty mounting up. Once into the saddle he had to clutch at the pommel with one hand to steady himself.

Clayburn's lips stretched back from his teeth as he watched from the shadow of a gray cedar. Fenton had told him Decolta had a reputation as a heavy drinker, as well as a wencher. But Decolta was further along than he'd expected, which would help. Perhaps Serina *had* given him a little extra luck. Clayburn was not superstitious; but he did not sneer at the possibility of an unexpected influence affecting one's luck. No gambler did.

He waited until Lieutenant Decolta rode away toward the fortress. Then, nudging the sorrel away from the cedar, he followed.

Halfway to the fortress, Clayburn kneed his horse to a faster pace. As he narrowed the distance between them he called out, "Lieutenant?"

Decolta drew to a halt, swaying as he turned in his saddle.

Clayburn stopped beside him, a slack, foolish smile on his face. "I went looking for you at the place you told me about." His voice was slurred and slow. "But you'd just left. . . ."

"You came too late," Decolta told him, his own voice thick and uncertain. "You should have come sooner . . . I had a new girl tonight. One of those who was brought here by force. . . .'' He grinned and licked his lips, pleased with himself. ''She cried at first. . . .''

''I got delayed,'' Clayburn told him. ''Stopped into a cantina for some drinks on the way . . . got into a fight. . . .''

''A fight?'' Decolta's frown was vague. ''Why?''

''Damned if I can remember,'' Clayburn slurred ruefully. ''Guess I had a little *too much* to drink. All I know is, suddenly I was in a fight with some man I never saw before. . . .''

Decolta peered at him more closely, blinking to get his eyes focused, seeing the bruises on Clayburn's face. ''You look as though you lost the fight.''

Clayburn scowled. ''Well . . . like I said, I had a little too much and. . . .''

''A gentleman should be able to hold his liquor, Captain.''

Clayburn got angry. ''That mean you think *I* can't? Listen, Lieutenant, I can drink you under the table any time I. . . .''

Decolta stiffened, and took the bait. ''I doubt that very much—Captain.''

''So . . . ? All right, Lieutenant, you're a gambling man. Tell you what. I got two bottles of brandy with me in these saddle bags. What d'you say we go to my room and each one of us starts drinking from one of those bottles. The first one of us to fall down owes the other one a full month's pay. Is it a bet?''

Decolta considered him, tempted, trying to think it out in his liquor-fumed brain.

Clayburn held onto his saddlehorn with both hands, leaning heavily for support. ''Well,'' he slurred, ''what do you say?''

''I say it is a bet,'' Decolta announced with stilted politeness, succeeding with an effort in getting the words out sharp and clear.

They rode the rest of the way to the fortress in silence. When they dismounted at the entrance gate, Clayburn stumbled and had to grab hold of his saddle to regain his balance. Decolta smiled.

Turning their permits to enter over to the officer in charge of the entrance guards, they took their horses to the stable.

Clayburn hung the saddlebags over his shoulder and made his way unsteadily toward the headquarters building. Beside him, Decolta concentrated on holding himself erect and dignified—and almost managed it. The guards inside the headquarters building let them pass without a word. They knew Decolta; and most of them had seen Clayburn with Dietrich. Leaving through the rear door, they made their way to the officers' building.

Inside his room, Clayburn put a match to the wall lamp, shut the door, and took the two bottles of brandy from his saddlebags. Moving heavily, he set the bottles down on the table. The bottle whose cork had a slight notch in it he set in front of himself. That was the bottle from which he had poured two-thirds of the brandy, refilling it with water.

Motioning Decolta to the other bottle with a wide, drunken gesture, Clayburn pulled the notched cork, tilted the mouth of his bottle between his teeth, and took several long swallows. He set the bottle down with a thump, gasping and blinking rapidly. The blinking made his eyes water satisfactorily. He wiped a hand across his eyes and waited, grinning slackly at Lieutenant Decolta.

Decolta pulled the cork from his bottle with deliberate dignity. He drank the way Clayburn had, from the bottle. And he drank a bit more than Clayburn had. When he set the bottle down gently he still stood rock-steady, feet braced slightly apart. He didn't gasp, and he didn't blink. His eyes had a hard shine to them.

Clayburn appeared a bit bothered by that. Angrily, he gulped from his bottle again, not setting it down until it was a third empty. He clutched at his edge of the table with one hand, shook his head slowly as though trying to clear fog from it.

Decolta leered at him, and drank an equal amount from his own bottle. This time when he lowered it his eyes were watering. They stared at each other, Clayburn continuing to hold onto the edge of the table. After a moment Decolta began to lean sideways a little, like a tree in a steady wind.

"May. . . ." Clayburn mumbled. He licked his lips and

got his vocal chords under some control. "Maybe . . . we should drink the rest sitting down?"

Lieutenant Decolta smiled a superior smiled. "If you wish. . . ." he slurred, and abruptly dropped into the chair on his side of the table.

Clayburn lowered himself to the seat of the other chair. Decolta watched him shut his eyes, open them again, and sit up a little straighter. They went on matching each other, drink for drink.

When both bottles were half empty, Clayburn seemed to go to sleep for a second. Then he shook himself, and rubbed the heel of his hand against his eyes, forcing them open. His fingers fumbled the bottle, got it up to his mouth. He took a long, long pull at it, put it down with a tired sigh, and looked at Decolta.

Decolta picked up his bottle. But he had to use both hands to do it. Some of the brandy ran down his chin and trickled on his uniform as he drank. He sagged back in his chair, clutching the bottle with both hands against his chest, his dazed eyes fastened on Clayburn.

Both bottles were almost empty when Lieutenant Decolta's head sank to one shoulder and stayed there. His eyes drooped shut. His hands, locked around the bottle, lowered limply to his lap and brandy trickled down his trouser leg. After a second, he began to make a small snoring noise.

Clayburn continued to slump in his own chair, watching the other man. After a time the vague look dissolved from his eyes. He leaned forward and prodded Decolta with the hard tip of a stiff forefinger. The lieutenant did not respond.

The slackness went out of Clayburn's face, leaving it hard and sullen. "Lieutenant!"

Decolta's eyes did not open. He went on snoring.

Clayburn stood up and went swiftly around the table to him. He fished in Decolta's pockets until he found what he wanted: the ring of keys. Decolta's snoring deepened.

Going to his door, Clayburn opened it, looking out cautiously. There was no one in the dim hall outside. He glanced back at Decolta. The lieutenant was out for the night. Of that he was certain. Despite the fact that his own brandy had been two-thirds water Clayburn had consumed enough of it to be feeling the effects. But he was rigidly in control of himself as he tugged off his boots, stepped out into the hall, and shut the door of his room behind him.

Moving soundlessly in his stockinged feet, he went to the locked door at the end of the hall. The second key he tried unlocked it. Clayburn sucked his lungs full, and quietly opened the door a few inches. Then he waited, poised tensely, listening. There was no sound on the other side of the door. He pushed it open a fraction wider and peered through. No one was in the corridor on the other side of it.

Clayburn let his breath out slow, stepped through, and closed the door. There was another closed door to his right. He put his ear to it. After a time he tried the door. It wasn't locked. Opening it, he looked inside. By the faint light coming in through the single window he made out a room much like his own. Squinting through the shadows, he made sure there was no one in the bed. Then he entered the room, crossing to the window. It looked down at the lamplit front of the building where Otero and Dietrich quartered.

Drawing back from the window, Clayburn went to a clothes closet and opened it. Reaching inside, he felt several gold-braided uniforms. He took one out, held it to the faint light coming through the window. The uniform was neatly pressed; the trousers razor-creased. This was Lieutenant Decolta's room. He confirmed this by examining the dress sword hanging from a wall peg. It was Decolta's.

Clayburn left the room. There were no other doors in the corridor this side of the door that was always kept locked. But down at the far end of the corridor was a stairwell leading down. He went to it, pausing at the top step. The stairwell led down into the passageway in the interior of the fortress wall. Clayburn wiped cold sweat from his eyes and started down the steps. He was almost to the bottom when he heard the sound of boots.

He froze, listening.

The sound came from the passageway, to his right. A single pair of boots—moving away from him. Clayburn wiped his damp palms on his Levi's and waited. The sound of the boots stopped. Then sounded again, coming back toward the bottom of the stairway.

Clayburn went up the steps swiftly and soundlessly; and dropped flat to the stone floor as he reached the top. The boots reached the bottom of the stairwell, paused. . . . He pressed himself against the stone floor, watching the top of the stairwell inches from his face, not breathing.

The boots moved on, to the left through the passageway running through the interior of the fortress's rear wall. Clayburn breathed again, carefully; but he did not budge. The sound he was listening to faded out. Still he did not move. Seconds went by. Then the sounds of the boots reached him again, coming back toward the bottom of the stairwell.

They reached there, paused, and then moved on to the right. Clayburn raised his head, looked down into the stairwell. He got his feet under him and moved silently and quickly down the steps to the bottom. Pressing against the wall there, he turned his head until one eye was looking around the corner, into the passageway to his right.

He found himself looking at the back of a trooper on sentry duty, moving away toward a shadowed archway at the end of the passage. Turning his head the other way, Clayburn looked into the short stretch of passageway to his left. He saw the door that led out into the courtyard. And further along the passage was a narrow flight of worn brick steps leading up to an opening in the top of the fortress wall.

Ducking back, Clayburn returned up the steps to the corridor. Went down it to the door. He'd learned all he could about one thing he'd had to know. There was more that had to be learned another way; a more dangerous way.

He went back into his own room, leaving his door open. Lieutenant Decolta was still snoring heavily in the chair. Slipping the ring of keys back in Decolta's pocket, he managed with some difficulty to drag the lieutenant's limp weight out of the chair. Carrying him in his arms, he went back down the hall, into the other corridor, and into Decolta's dark room.

The lieutenant grunted when he was dumped on his bed. But he did not waken from his liquor-drugged sleep. Clay-

burn left the room and went back through the corridor door,
shutting it behind him. There was no way to lock it from the
other side and still leave the keys with Decolta. But that didn't
bother Clayburn too much. The condition the lieutenant
would be in when he woke in the morning, he'd just figure
he'd forgotten to lock it. And he wasn't likely to bring up the
omission with anyone else.

Shutting the door of his own room, Clayburn turned out
the lamp and stretched out on his bed to wait. One thing he
hadn't found in the forbidden stretch at the other end of the
corridor was a way down to the interior of the ground floor.
So there was only one way left to find out what was below
the projection that ran the length of the building wall below
his window. . . .

He waited for half an hour. Long enough for anyone who'd
noticed the light in his room to assume he'd gone to sleep.
Then he rose from the bed and moved tensely through the
darkened room to his window. Standing a little back from it,
he looked down into the courtyard. Neither of the two sentries in front of the treasure-house door, and none of the
three-man gun crew, were looking up. There was no reason
why they should—except that men standing guard duty sometimes shifted a little or moved their heads just to ease the
cramping monotony of standing still so long.

Shifting to one side, Clayburn viewed the three sentries in
sight on top of the rear wall of the fortress. None of them
were looking in his direction. Again, there was no reason
why they should. Their job was to look in the other direction,
out into the darkness of the canyon on the other side of the
river rushing past the rear wall.

Clayburn moved to the window, rested a hip on the lower
sill. He was in plain sight now. But none of the five men in
the courtyard below glanced upward, as they would have
done if they'd noticed him there. And the three sentries on
the fortress wall continued to gaze out in the opposite direction.

Swinging one leg over the sill, Clayburn rested his other
foot on the sill and grasped the outer corners of the window.
Still not one of the men in the courtyard below raised his

head. Clayburn stood up outside the window, his stockinged feet braced apart on the lower sill. Going up on his toes and stretching his arms above him, he was just able to reach the edge of the flat roof. His fingers clamped down on it. His shoulder muscles bunched, straining against the material of his shirt as he hauled himself straight up until he was looking across the dark-shadowed top of the roof.

Without pausing he swung a leg up, hooked his foot on the roof edge, and heaved himself up onto the top of the roof. As soon as he was stretched out flat on it he looked down again. The men in front of the treasure house had not noticed him. Clayburn snaked backward from the roof edge until he could no longer see the bottom of the courtyard—or the men in it. Now, for a time, all he would have to worry about was those three sentries on top of the fortress wall with their backs to him.

He kept his eyes on them as he inched across the roof on his belly. The night shadows offered the only form of cover. Clayburn followed a changing route that took advantage of these. He angled toward the roof of the next building—the one siding the courtyard across from the fortress wall.

He was almost to it when one of the sentries on the wall turned around and looked in his direction.

SIXTEEN

Clayburn became a motionless patch of dark shadow on the roof.

Anyone looking for a man on that roof would have noticed that his still form was not quite like the other shadows. But the sentry was not looking for anything. He was merely moving to relieve his boredom. He stretched his arms and gazed aimlessly across the roofs inside the fortress. Clayburn lay flat and watched him, his breathing slow and shallow, his heart thudding against the surface of the roof under him.

The sentry stretched again and looked down into the courtyard. He turned his head and spat, wiped his mouth with the back of a hand. Then he turned all the way and resumed his vigil over the canyon beyond the wall.

Clayburn's eyes closed and opened. The tip of his tongue crawled between his teeth and withdrew. He resumed inching his way forward with his elbows and toes, the rest of him raised just a hair above the surface over which he moved.

The adjacent roof was a continuation of the one over the officers' building, without a break. Clayburn crawled its length, sticking to the shadows in the middle of it. When he was almost to the far end of this other roof he paused, studied the sentries on the fortress wall, then shifted direction. Snaking to the inner edge of the roof, he paused again. Then pulled himself forward another inch and looked over the edge.

Now the roof of the treasure house was below him. He looked down on the cannon and the five men guarding the treasure-house door. Then across the courtyard at the officers' building from which he'd come. Form here he could see his window, the wall projection under his window—and what was below that projection.

There were no windows in the lower floor of the building in which his room was located. And no doors. But there was an open archway, leading under the officers' building to the rear of the building in which Otero and Dietrich lived. In one inner wall of the archway, halfway through it, was a closed door.

Now Clayburn knew what he'd crawled the roof to find out. Most of it. There was one item left to be learned. To learn it he would have to wait where he was. If his calculations were correct, he wouldn't have to wait long.

The waiting stretched to almost half an hour. Then it came: the changing of the guard.

Clayburn saw the door inside the archway open. Ten troopers emerged from it, marching away and vanishing into the rear of the building housing Otero and Dietrich. Nine more came out, turning in the opposite direction, toward Clayburn into the courtyard. He watched these replace the five in front of the treasure house, the three on the wall, and the one inside the wall.

He held himself rigid, flat down on the roof, pressing down as though trying to merge with it. He was scarcely breathing now. In the process of making the change, the guards were looking in many directions—some of them glancing by chance directly at the spot where he lay. But none of them were looking for a man; so none of them noticed that the dark patch he formed on the roof was slightly different from the other night shadows.

The five men relieved of their duty in front of the treasure house, the sentry from inside the wall, and the three from the top of the wall, marched away across the courtyard. They went halfway through the archway and filed into the door in its inner wall. Ten troopers appeared from the other end of the archway and also vanished inside the door, shutting it behind them.

Now Clayburn knew as much as he could know. The

ground floor of the officers' building contained the quarters for this special guard unit. And that door inside the archway was apparently the only means by which these special guards could get into—or out of—those sealed-off quarters.

Clayburn gave some thought to the cannon in front of the treasure house. As near as he could judge from this angle, it was lined up almost exactly with the archway across the courtyard from it.

The changing of the guard was over. But Clayburn continued to lie where he was, not moving, giving the new men time to settle into the mind-numbing monotony of their guard duty.

He remained motionless for an entire hour. Then he inched backward until the men in the courtyard were out of sight. Turning his head to keep the three wall sentries in view all the way, he began retracing his route. He belly-crawled to the roof of the officers' building, angled toward a point that would be directly over the window of his room.

One of the wall sentries turned his head to say something to one of the others. Clayburn stopped moving. The other sentry turned and replied. Clayburn held himself in with a fierce effort, waiting out their conversation. It seemed to go on and on.

Finally they seemed to run their subject into the ground. When all three sentries once more had their backs to him, Clayburn snaked the rest of the way to the roof edge above his window. The five men in the courtyard below were now visible to him again. And he would be visible to any one of them who chanced to look up. This was the most dangerous part of all.

Clayburn slid each leg forward until all of him was stretched out along the roof edge. He drew a slow breath. Both hands closed on the edge. The rest was done in one swift, combined movement. He swung over the edge, lowering himself full-length, hanging by his hands. The instant his stockinged feet touched the lower sill of his window he released his hand-hold, squatted down, and dropped through the window to the floor of his room in a low crouch.

Instantly he twisted around and rose up from the crouch

just enough to look out over the sill. None of the guards in the courtyard or on the wall had changed position. No one had seen him.

Backing away from the window, he kept to the crouch until he was in the middle of his darkened room. Then he stood up. His legs began to tremble uncontrollably. He was covered with sweat from head to foot. His clothes were drenched with it. He raised both hands and pressed them hard against his eyes, pulled them slowly down his face. Then he stripped off the wet, clinging clothes and went unsteadily to the wash-basin on the bureau.

He sank his face into the cool water in the basin, kept it there for a full minute, and came up gasping for air. Cupping water with both hands, he poured it on top of his head, kneaded it into his scalp. He used more of the water to wash the sweat from the rest of him, got the towel from the hook beside the bureau and dried himself all over.

Then he went to the bed, fell facedown on top of it, and allowed himself to pass out.

Lieutenant Decolta looked pretty bad the next morning when he came to Clayburn's room. There were dark bruises under his bloodshot eyes, and his face was puffy.

Clayburn, dressing for breakfast, eyed him and shook his head. "If it's any consolation to you, I feel as rotten as you look."

Decolta managed a sheepish smile. "I only wish to know. . . ." He hesitated, cleared his throat. "I . . . ah . . . remember our bet, but . . . who won?"

"Damned if I know, Lieutenant. The last I can remember of last night we were both still drinking. The next thing I knew, I came to an hour ago, still sitting in that chair over there."

Decolta brightened a bit, as much as he could with the hangover clamping its hold on him. "Then it must be that *I* got up after you passed out in the chair, and walked back to my room without realizing it. . . . This means, does it not, that I am the winner?"

"I'm afraid so," Clayburn conceded ruefully. "I owe you

a whole month's pay. Remind me never to try matching drinks with you again.''

"I warned you," Decolta reminded him proudly.

"Yes, you did. Want to go in town again tonight? You can introduce me to some of those ladies you mentioned."

Decolta touched his throbbing temple with shaky fingers. "I do not think I will feel quite up to it tonight," he mumbled, and left the room with a heavy tread.

After breakfast Clayburn returned to his room and stretched out on his bed again to soak up more sleep. It was almost noon when one of Otero's officers came with word that Dietrich wanted to see him.

Dietrich stood examining the wall map when Clayburn entered his office after being announced by one of the four ever-present bodyguards. He asked without taking his eyes off the map, "Where have you been all morning, Captain?"

"Catching up on my sleep."

Dietrich turned from the map. "I have been. . . ." Then he got a good look at Clayburn, and his bright blue eyes narrowed. "What happened to you?"

Clayburn touched his bruised face and shrugged. "Had too much to drink in town last night, and got into a fight."

"A fight—with whom?" Dietrich demanded sharply.

Clayburn grinned crookedly. "I was too drunk to remember."

Dietrich continued to stare at him, not liking it. Not liking it at all. "What I know of you is from your reputation alone. I did not know from that that you were a drunkard. Or is that something new?"

"Don't worry about my reputation," Clayburn snapped back angrily. "I never drink on duty. And what I drink has never affected the performance of my duty."

"I hope that proves to be true." Dietrich's voice had a cold, nasty edge to it. "For *your* sake, Captain. I am expecting the report on the village I told you about tomorrow morning. If the rumor of arms hidden there is true, you will leave immediately to execute all its inhabitants. Understand?"

Clayburn nodded. "I'll be ready."

"You had better be. And understand this, too, Captain. . . . Consider it an order: You will do no drinking tonight."

"I won't," Clayburn agreed flatly.

Dietrich went on looking at him with displeasure for several seconds. Then he sat down behind his desk and said: "I have been giving your suggestion more thought. A stockade between the guns and the entrance gate *is* necessary. I'm placing you in charge of building it. Now. You can request as many men as you need to get it done, from the officer in charge of the gate."

"All right." Clayburn turned to leave.

He was almost to the door when Dietrich said sharply: "Captain!"

Clayburn turned to look at him. Dietrich leaned back in his chair and said softly, "I had hoped that you would have something to tell me."

"Such as. . . ?"

"What did General Otero have to say to you yesterday . . . in your room?"

Clayburn smiled—to keep any other expression out of his face. So one of Otero's own men was a spy for Dietrich. Maybe even one of the general's bodyguards. . . . That was an unpleasant bit of news. It meant that any time he went to Otero, it would be reported to Dietrich. How much damage that did would depend on how *fast* it was reported.

"Otero didn't have much to say, Colonel. Just that he'd show his appreciation of my loyalty, after the fighting was over."

Dietrich's expression didn't change. "What do you think he meant by that?"

Clayburn continued to smile. "I figure he meant that he'd be pleased if my loyalty was to him—more than to you."

"I see. . . . And how do you feel about this?"

Clayburn shrugged a shoulder. "I spent years getting the Apaches under control. Saw some damn good fighting men killed doing it—only to have the politicians in the Indian Bureau ruin everything we'd fought for." His eyes met Dietrich's. "For a change I wouldn't mind seeing the politicians wind up on the bottom. I wouldn't mind that at all, Colonel."

Dietrich's face defrosted slightly. "I think we understand each other, Captain."

Clayburn spent the rest of the day getting the stockade built between the gate and the cannons. At one point late in the afternoon he saw Joe Fenton stroll by. They made a point of not looking at each other. It was almost dusk when Dietrich came out, inspected what he had done, and approved.

On the way back to the headquarters building with Dietrich, Clayburn mentioned that his weapons were still out at the entrance to the canyon.

"I'll need them when I take that detail out tomorrow. I'd like to get them now. Rode through a lot of dust with them. They could use a cleaning and oiling."

There was nothing about such a request to make Dietrich suspect anything. In his office he wrote out an order for Clayburn to pick up his arms and bring them into the fortress.

Clayburn pocketed it and went to the door.

"Remember," Dietrich said behind him, "no drinking tonight."

Clayburn turned and looked at Dietrich, and the four bodyguards. All he hoped now was that Dietrich would show up within range at the right time tonight. If he did, those bodyguards wouldn't be much help in keeping him alive.

"No drinking," he agreed quietly, and headed for his room.

After supper that night he caught up with Lieutenant Decolta outside the officers' dining room.

"You look like you're feeling better," he told him. It was true. Decolta's appearance had improved considerably during the day, though there were still those dark smears under his eyes.

Decolta nodded. "Better. But not enough for more. . . ."

"I had enough last night to suit me for awhile myself," Clayburn said. "Come to my room and I'll write a note that I owe you a month's pay."

Decolta made a small gesture of protest. "Your word is good enough for me."

Clayburn insisted. "I'll feel better about owing it to you if the debt's in writing."

Decolta shrugged. "If you wish. . . ." He accompanied Clayburn to his room.

Inside, Clayburn shut the door, crossed the night-darkened room to the lamp. There was a heavy brass candle holder on the bureau beside it. Clayburn dug into his pocket, pulled his hand out empty. "Damn. . . . Got a match?"

Lieutenant Decolta came across the room behind him. Clayburn picked up the brass candle holder and spun around, slamming it across the side of Decolta's skull with all his strength.

Decolta fell sideways across the bed. He did not move again. After a few moments he stopped breathing.

Clayburn put down the candle holder. His nostrils were pinched and his eyes dull. But he felt no qualm. Not about exterminating this man—who took his pleasure from women who'd been taken prisoner and forced to submit.

Digging into the dead man's pocket, he got the ring of keys, slipped it into his own pocket. He dragged the limp body off the mattress, shoved it out of sight under the bed. Then he got his denim work jacket from his saddlebags and started for the door.

It had begun now. Before the night was over he and the others would be out of here with the loot—or dead.

SEVENTEEN

Clayburn rode to the canyon entrance and requisitioned his weapons with the note Dietrich had scrawled. He buckled on his gunbelt and slid the carbine into his saddle scabbard. The knife in the soft buckskin sheath he strapped once more to the inside of his left forearm, pulling the sleeve of his shirt and denim jacket down to conceal it. Then he mounted the sorrel again and rode back into the town.

Leaving the horse with Roa, he went through the corridor and down the steps, knocking at the cellar door. When the door opened the first man he saw by the lamplight inside was Brazos Williams. The second was a blond man with yellow eyebrows and mustache, whom it took him a split-second to register as Juan Ramirez.

Juan smiled and touched his dyed hair self-consciously. "You can stop gawking at me, Clay. Had to do *something* so I could get in without being recognized."

"Easier for me," Brazos put in. "None of 'em know me by sight yet."

Clayburn stepped in and shut the door. Looked past Juan and Brazos to Latigo and Fenton—then back to Juan. He was ten pounds thinner and his face was painfully gaunt.

"You look like hell," Clayburn told him flatly.

Juan pretended to misunderstand. "Never did like a mustache, myself. I'll shave it off afterwards. Everything ready in there?"

"As ready as it'll ever be. But are *you*?"

"If I wasn't, I wouldn't be here. I didn't come to foul things up."

"I know that," Clayburn said. "Just want to make sure you're ready for all of it. That jump alone's bound to open up that wound of yours."

Juan shrugged. "So I'll bleed."

Clayburn found himself grinning at him.

Fenton growled, "What're you tryin' to talk him out of it for? Now there's five of us, we at least got a chance."

"Means we'll need more of those permits to enter the fortress," Clayburn mentioned.

Latigo smiled. "We *have* them—all three."

That meant three of Dietrich's men were already stretched out under bushes somewhere outside town. Killed for the permits they carried. That was the one thing about those permits that made this operation possible: the only name on any of them was Dietrich's. Anyone who had one could use it.

Brazos distributed five small packages: candles and matches, sealed in water-tight oilskin. Each man stuck one in his pocket. These would provide light through the caves under the mountains.

Latigo got a supply of empty canvas bags from a corner of the room and turned them over to Clayburn. A length of rawhide linked each pair. And each bag had a drawstring sewed in, so it could be closed securely at the top after it was filled. Clayburn stuffed the bags out of sight inside the shoulders of his denim work jacket and in its pockets.

Then they settled down to wait. It would have to be a long wait—long enough to give Dietrich and everyone else inside the fortress who wasn't on duty time to get deep into sleep. Clayburn passed the time telling them—in detail—exactly what he had learned the previous night; exactly what they were going to run up against, and exactly what they were going to do about it.

It was two hours past midnight when the five of them reached the gate of the fortress. Fenton went first through the small door in the gate. Clayburn followed, showing his authorization for bringing in his weapons to the officer in charge. He nodded toward the others. "Dietrich sent me to fetch these three."

The officer inspected the permits presented to him by Juan, Latigo and Brazos—and passed them through.

Inside the fortress, they left their horses at the stables and headed back down the parade grounds. They stuck to the night shadows of walls and buildings—and avoided the main headquarters. There were too many guards on duty at all times in there for them to get through it. But the armory room down at the other end of the parade grounds was another matter.

Clayburn led the way in, carrying the carbine in his left hand. There was an armed guard just inside the doorway. Beyond him was a wall that prevented access to the rest of the armory room. In the wall was a locked door, and an iron-barred little window. The night man in charge of weapons sat behind that barred window, on the other side of the wall.

"Turning my guns in," Clayburn told the guard inside the doorway.

The guard nodded, letting Clayburn move on past him. Fenton came in the doorway at the same time. The guard, recognizing him, started to say something—and then saw the other three coming in behind Fenton.

Fenton reached inside his shirt and pulled out a Colt—the one that had belonged to Morales. The guard's mouth shut with a snap, started to open again. The Colt thudded down on top of his skull. He dropped as though his legs had been cut out from under him. Fenton caught him as Juan caught his falling rifle. Latigo snatched the Colt from the guard's holster as Brazos moved up behind Clayburn. The man behind the barred window sat frozen in his chair, gaping into the dark mouth of the carbine that Clayburn held trained on him.

"The key," Clayburn whispered.

It took a moment for the man to get his hands moving. He groped for the key, found it, and passed it through the bars. Clayburn took it with his left hand, passed it back to Brazos. He kept the carbine pointing through the bars while Brazos unlocked the door and went through with the others; Fenton pulling the body of the guard in after him. When Juan appeared behind the man on the other side of the barred window, Clayburn withdrew the carbine and followed them into the back section of the armory, locking the door behind him.

By the time he turned from the door the man in charge of weapons was sprawled out on the floor beside the guard. And Latigo was at the back door. He opened it a crack and peeked out, then shoved it all the way open and stepped through to the sentry stationed outside. There was a soft thump—and then Latigo was dragging the unconscious sentry inside.

Clayburn went to the rear doorway and stationed himself there, watching the shadowed passageways outside while the others finished arming themselves with loaded rifles and Colts from the armory's ample supplies. Fenton came up with the best find: a double-barreled sawed-off shotgun. He came out with it in one hand and a rifle in the other. Clayburn led them away toward the officers' building. Following the route along which they'd be least likely to be seen.

Every second used up increased their danger now. Not that there was any chance of the men they'd left in the armory giving the alarm. They'd been hit hard and with purpose. If any of them ever came to, it wouldn't be before morning. But sooner or later someone was bound to enter the armory and find them the way they'd been left. . . .

The front of the officers' building was unlighted. Clayburn managed to lead the others around the corner and through deep shadow into the doorway without being spotted by any of the sentries in the area. They went swiftly up the winding stairs to the second floor, and down the hall.

Pausing briefly in front of his room, Clayburn nodded to Brazos. Carrying his rifle in his left hand, Brazos slipped inside the room, closing the door behind him. Clayburn moved on with the other three men to the locked door, opened it with Decolta's key.

Fenton was the last man through. And it was Fenton whose elbow bumped sharply against the wall as he closed the door, causing him to drop the sawed-off shotgun. Clayburn was already to the top of the steps leading down into the inner passageway of the fortress wall when he heard the shotgun bounce off the stone flooring of the corridor behind him.

It was a sound that carried. Fenton snatched up the shotgun immediately, but it was too late for that to help. Down in the passageway to the right of the bottom of the stairs, the sound of the sentry's footsteps ceased. Then sounded again, coming back toward the stairwell.

There was only one way left to cope with him. Clayburn slid the knife from inside his sleeve, palmed it in his right hand, and drew the hand back—poised for the throw.

The sentry came into view at the foot of the stairs. He was turning to look up when Clayburn whipped his right hand forward and down. The sentry had his mouth partway open and his rifle halfway up when the slim steel blade drove between his ribs into his heart. He made a small sound in his throat and fell heavily. What was much worse was the clatter of his rifle on the lower steps beside him.

Clayburn went down the stairs fast, stepped over the sentry into the passageway. It was empty. He looked toward the steps that led up to the top of the wall, waiting to see if the noise had alerted any of the three men up there.

When two minutes went by without anyone coming down those steps, Clayburn went on through the passage to the door leading out to the courtyard. Finding the key that fitted, he unlocked the door. But did not open it.

He returned to the others waiting on the steps that led down into the passageway. Only Juan noticed that he stepped over the sentry without looking down. Noticed, too, the drawn, ugly look of Clayburn's face; and that he did not pause to retrieve his knife.

There was no need for words between them now. Each knew what his job was. Juan, Fenton and Latigo went down into the passageway to wait. Clayburn continued on up the steps to the corridor. It was not until he was at the top, and the others were out of sight, that he leaned against the wall. He stayed that way for several moments, eyes shut tight, fighting down the sickness that had risen inside him.

Then he pushed away from the wall and moved on. Their margin of luck was thinning out with blinding speed by now.

He went to his room and entered it. Brazos, crouched beside the window, looked up quickly, then resumed his vigil. Clayburn put his carbine down beside Brazos, drew his Colt from the holster and slipped it inside his shirt, where the bulge of it was hidden by one side of his open jacket. Unbuckling his gunbelt, he tossed it on the bed. Then he went out of his room and out of the building; across the square to Otero's living quarters. And Dietrich's.

At the entrance to the building he announced himself and his purpose. Two of the sentries barred his way with their crossed rifles while another went inside to consult with the officer on duty. Clayburn waited in the smoky yellowish glow of the two kerosene lamps hung from wall hooks on either side of the entrance.

The officer who emerged knew Clayburn—as Captain Cullen. They had spoken to each other briefly at mealtimes. He faced Clayburn uncertainly. "You wish to see the general—*now*?"

Clayburn nodded. "Tell him it concerns what we spoke about yesterday. And that it's urgent. He'll understand."

The officer hesitated, frowning. "But to wake him at this time of night. . . ."

"I'll take full responsibility for that." Clayburn choked down the nervous anger at the time being wasted. "The general won't mind. Believe me."

The officer continued to hesitate, sucking his lower lip between his teeth. Finally he shrugged. "*Your* responsibility," he reminded, and motioned Clayburn inside.

Clayburn followed him across a large entrance hall, into one of several corridors leading from it, past the room where he had dined with Dietrich, up a wide staircase and down another wide, lamp-lit corridor. He wondered where Dietrich's quarters were in relation to Otero's, but did not ask. The corridor led about halfway through to the rear of the building, ending against a large door with ornamental brasswork on it.

There were two sentries guarding the door. They stood stiffly at attention as their officer went between them, had one last spasm of hesitation, and then knocked gently at the door. It was opened from the inside by another armed guard.

The officer glanced back to Clayburn. "Your responsibility," he repeated.

Clayburn nodded.

"Wait here." The officer heaved a quick, nervous sigh and went in, closing the door.

Clayburn remained in the corridor, the two sentries staring blankly at him while he stared blankly at a dull spot in the door's brasswork. He was wondering if the spy Dietrich had among Otero's men would decide to wait until morning to report this night visit. Or if he would consider it unusual enough to warrant waking Dietrich to inform him of it immediately. It was a gut-clenching point to worry about.

The door opened. The officer motioned for him to enter, not looking happy about it. "The general is *very* angry," he whispered tightly as Clayburn went past him, into a large ornately furnished sitting room.

"He won't be," Clayburn assured him.

The officer looked extremely dubious about that as he went out, leaving Clayburn alone in the sitting room. Not quite alone. Beside the guard inside the door to the corridor, there was one of Otero's bodyguards in front of another door on the other side of the room.

Clayburn stood stiffly beside a heavy, brocade-covered sofa, and waited.

The other door opened and Otero appeared in slippers and red silk dressing gown, his face softly wrinkled and his eyes blurry with sleep. "Well?" he rasped angrily.

Clayburn looked at the two guards, then again at Otero. "This is something we should discuss in private, General."

"At this time of night?" Otero's crankiness at being dragged out of a sound sleep was making this more difficult than Clayburn had anticipated.

"What I have to tell you won't wait. It's something you should know about—now. I think you and I understood each other yesterday, General." Clayburn got all the quiet significance he could into his voice. "What I have to tell you concerns something that's about to happen. By tomorrow it'll be too late for you."

That was as close as he could get to warning Otero that Dietrich was planning something immediate against him, without saying it out loud in front of the two guards—either of whom might be in Dietrich's employ.

Otero scowled at Clayburn, muttered something under his breath, and then gestured for him to come with him. Clayburn followed him through the door, closed it behind him. They were in a small study, not the bedroom. For that, Clayburn was grateful. From what one of the officers had said at dinner that evening, Otero had a mistress stashed away somewhere in here.

Clayburn was registering two other closed doors in the room when Otero turned to face him.

"Very well, Captain. We are alone."

"Yes." Clayburn drew the gun from inside his shirt and placed its muzzle against the center of Otero's chest. "One yell," he whispered, "and you're a dead general."

Otero blinked at him stupidly. He looked down at the gun; at Clayburn's thumb on the hammer, ready to cock it back.

When he looked up at Clayburn again his eyes were narrow, and not at all stupid. "Think well, Captain. . . . Whatever you intend, you cannot possibly get away alive afterwards."

"You'll make sure I *do* get away alive," Clayburn told him. "This commits me. From here on, no matter what I do or don't do, I'll be killed if I'm caught. So it can't possibly go any worse for me if I kill you first. And if you do anything—anything at all—to help me get caught, I *will* kill you. Be very sure of that."

His voice was very soft, and the deadliness of it shook Otero. So did what he saw in Clayburn's eyes. Fear tugged at the corners of his tight mouth. He tried to swallow and seemed to find it difficult to do.

"I'm after some of the jewels in that treasure room of yours," Clayburn went on in the same soft, deadly voice. "You'll do everything you can think of to help me get them. And to make sure nothing happens along the way to raise an alarm. Those jewels won't be any use to you if you're dead. Just keep thinking about what you want most—to stop me, or to stay alive.''

Otero seemed to find some horrid fascination in Clayburn's eyes. Like a toad staring at a poisonous snake coiled to strike. His head jerked in a frightened nod. "What . . . do you want me to do?''

"Start thinking for yourself, General. Remember—your life hangs on my getting away with this.''

Otero's face had become the color of lead. "The keys . . .'' He had trouble forming the words and getting them out. ". . . the keys to the treasure house are in this desk.''

Clayburn nodded toward a door behind the desk. "Where does that go?''

"My bedroom,'' Otero whispered in a fright-squeezed voice.

"And that one over there?''

"To a stairway leading down to the rear door of the building.''

"And out to the courtyard. . . .''

"Yes.''

Clayburn prodded him with the gun. "Get the keys.''

Otero looked desperately toward the door to his bedroom. "Let me get dressed first and . . .''

"No. There's no time. You'll go as you are—*now*.''

Otero almost stumbled over his feet getting to the desk. From a drawer he took out two keys—one large and the other smaller—linked by a gold ring.

"Put them in your pocket,'' Clayburn ordered. "That's it.'' He stuck the gun into his belt where it was hidden by the flap of his denim jacket, and hooked the thumb of his right hand on his belt buckle, close to it.

"Let's go,'' he said softly. "The rest should be easy for you. Just think about all the ways you can trick me between here and there—and about what the bullet will feel like when it breaks your spine.''

They went out by way of the back door together, Otero being very careful to keep in step with Clayburn. The guard outside stood rooted in position as they went past, making a point of not reacting to the sight of his general going out in slippers and dressing gown. It was the same with the others they passed, going down the back steps and out through the rear door of the building.

Otero's face was utterly devoid of expression as they walked through the archway together, out onto the courtyard. He was concentrating on doing absolutely nothing that might make Clayburn get nervous with the gun concealed inches from his hand.

The sentries and gun crew in front of the treasure house went rigid as Otero appeared. They remained at attention, staring straight ahead of them, while Otero and Clayburn went between them to the heavy door. Light from the kerosene lamps hanging on either side of the door glinted on the keys Otero took from the pocket of his dressing gown. He inserted the large one in the lock, turned it with a snap, and pushed the door open.

Inside, Otero took a lamp down from the wall and turned to Clayburn with it, wordlessly. He found it difficult to speak because of the dry tightness in his throat; and words weren't necessary. Clayburn got a match from his pocket with his left hand. He rasped his thumbnail across it, lit the lamp, and shut the door on the courtyard. Otero carried the lamp to an inner door, opened it with the smaller key.

And then they were inside the treasure room.

Clayburn ignored the piles of gold and silver, the great sacks that obviously contained coins. "Where's the jewelry?"

Otero moved slowly, reluctantly, to an enormous chest. Putting the lamp down on the stone floor, he seized the handle set in the lid of the chest and dragged it open.

The result was dazzling. The chest was crammed to the top with a fantastic display of jewelry encrusted with precious gems that glistened and winked and gleamed in the lamplight.

Clayburn wasted no time in admiring the display. Shrugging out of the denim jacket, he dropped the rawhide-joined canvas bags from his shoulders. He pulled the other two pairs of canvas bags from the pockets of the jacket, tossed them at Otero's feet.

Then he drew the revolver from inside his shirt. "Start filling them." The dark round mouth of the gun steadied on Otero's face. "And don't be slow about it. Every second counts. For both of us."

Otero stared into the mouth of the gun. "Be careful. . . ." he whispered weakly. "If that goes off . . . by accident . . . the guards will hear the noise and. . . ."

Clayburn smiled wolfishly. "And you'll be all finished dying by the time they get here."

Otero snatched up one pair of canvas bags and got to work.

Otero's bodyguard gave Dietrich what information he had: Captain Cullen had gone into General Otero's private quarters alone to talk to him about something urgent that had come up. As far as he knew, the captain and Otero were still in there together.

Dietrich stood stiffly in his waiting room, and scowled at the man without really seeing him. He was looking at something else, inside his head.

A secret conference between Captain Cullen and Otero could only mean one thing: they were planning something against him.

The suddenness of this conference, in the middle of the night, could mean that whatever they were planning was about to happen.

"Wait here," he snapped at Otero's bodyguard. "I will be ready in a moment."

Dietrich strode back into his bedroom, quickly got into his clothes and pulled on his boots. And strapped on his gunbelt.

EIGHTEEN

Dietrich entered Otero's quarters with his face set like stone and his right hand on the grip of his holstered gun. Trailed closely by his own special bodyguards, he moved purposefully through the entire suite of rooms, searching. By the time he came back out of the last one, the bedroom, his expression was changing to one of probing thoughtfulness.

They weren't here—and they hadn't left Otero's quarters by way of the front door. Dietrich went to the rear door and yanked it open, questioning the guard outside sharply.

The guard nodded, pointing toward the stairs leading down to the rear of the building.

Dietrich gazed in that direction for several seconds in silence. Perhaps Otero and Captain Cullen had gone to muster the special guards to help in their plan. Perhaps—it might be something quite different that was going on. But just in case. . . .

Dietrich sent one of his bodyguards off toward the main parade grounds to rouse his own men with orders to stand ready for trouble. With the other three bodyguards, he headed down the rear stairs.

He could not be sure what he would find at the bottom, and so he moved cautiously. He found nothing wrong there, nor along the corridor leading to the back door. Nor out in the archway to the courtyard.

Halfway through the archway Dietrich paused beside the door to the special guards' quarters. Out in the courtyard, all was quiet. The two sentries and the three-man gun crew stood at their posts in front of the treasure house, as always. Dietrich experienced a cold, crawling sensation in the small of his back. It was possible that Otero and Captain Cullen were inside the quarters of the special guards here, at this minute. . . . But it was beginning to dawn on Dietrich that there was another possibility. One he hadn't considered before.

Motioning to two of his bodyguards, he sent them to find out if Otero and the other had gone in either possible direction through the courtyard—into the wall; or the treasure house. Dietrich himself remained at the door in the archway with the remaining bodyguard, watching the other two move out into the courtyard.

Inside the treasure house, Otero finished lugging the last of the crammed-full pairs of canvas bags from the strong-room, setting it down by the door to the courtyard. Then he straightened and backed off a step, his frightened eyes on Clayburn and the gun in Clayburn's hand. Otero was not the man he had been. The self-assurance and self-importance no longer showed.

Clayburn picked up one pair of jewel-stuffed canvas bags. He got the length of rawhide that joined the two bags across the back of his neck, so the bags hung at his sides where each could be held secure in the crook of an arm. He looked at the other four pairs of filled bags, then at the closed door to the courtyard.

There was no ruse that could get them through the rest of it. Between that door and the outside of the fortress, it was going to have to be a battle all the way.

He gestured at Otero with the gun. "Open the door and step out in front of me—slow."

Otero's movements were sluggish as he obeyed. There was a slack, dazed look to his face. He pulled the door open and started through with Clayburn right behind him.

Looking past Otero, Clayburn saw Dietrich's two bodyguards coming straight across the courtyard—and beyond them Dietrich and the other bodyguard deep inside the archway.

Clayburn reacted instantly. His left forearm slid around

Otero's neck to hold him in place. His right fist brought the gun up under Otero's armpit, firing it as the two bodyguards in the courtyard went for their own weapons. The bullet punched into the chest of the bodyguard on the right, crumpling him to the ground.

The sound of the shot triggered an instant explosion of violence that engulfed the entire courtyard area. Within several seconds of that sound, many things happened at the same time:

Brazos leaned out of the second-story window and fired his rifle down into the courtyard. The other bodyguard there had his gun out when he took the bullet in the back of his skull, pitching forward on his face.

The door in the base of the fortress wall flung open and Juan and Latigo erupted out of it, both with a Colt in each hand—letting go with a roaring barrage that was joined by Brazo's rapid rifle fire from the upper window—pouring a hail of lead into the two sentries and three artillerymen in the courtyard.

Dietrich whipped his revolver from its holster before the blast of Clayburn's gun faded. He fired through the archway, straight at the treasure-house doorway. It was impossible for him to hit the little of Clayburn that could be seen behind Otero, with a hand gun at that distance. Even as he fired, Clayburn realized that that was not what Dietrich intended.

Dietrich fired twice in rapid succession. Both of the heavy slugs struck Otero in the heart area, pounding him backward against Clayburn.

Clayburn returned Dietrich's fire. But Otero's sagging dead weight spoiled his aim. The shot missed. Before he could try for another Dietrich shoved open the door to the special guards' quarters and dodged inside, followed by his remaining bodyguard, yelling the alarm.

At the same time Fenton popped up into view atop the fortress wall, squeezing both triggers of the sawed-off shotgun at the three sentries there. It was point-blank range. The concentrated double blast got all three of them, smashing them off the wall.

And then, abruptly, there was no one in sight left alive to shoot at. The attack had been too unexpected, swift, and coordinated for the men of the fortress to do anything about it. They had not even been able to slow the operation by a split-second as they died.

Juan and Latigo were already rushing past Clayburn into the doorway of the treasure house. Brazos was slipping through the window to the wall projection, dropping from it to the courtyard. He landed on both feet, staggered, and then came sprinting across toward the treasure house. Clayburn grabbed one of the kerosene lamps from its wall hook beside the door and moved over next to the cannon. He stood there with the lamp ready in one hand and the Colt in his other, watching the archway. His calculation of the previous night had been correct; the cannon and the archway were in a direct line with each other.

Atop the wall, Fenton began firing a rifle at something down at the other end of the wall. Juan and Latigo came out of the treasure house, each with two filled bags hanging at his sides from the rawhide strip across the back of his neck. The two of them carried a third pair of loot-heavy bags between them. As they headed for the door in the wall, Brazos went past Clayburn into the treasure house.

At that moment rifle-armed troopers began pouring out of the special guards' quarters into the archway, turning toward the courtyard.

Clayburn smashed the kerosene lamp across the cannon's fuse hole.

The troopers in the lead inside the archway saw him do it, and understood what it meant even as the licking kerosene flames ignited the powder fuse. They twisted around desperately and began shoving back the way they'd come in frenzied panic, tangling with the men behind them. There were about nine of them in the archway when the cannon let go with a shattering roar. The archway became filled with slashing chain-shot and flying shards of scrap-iron; with screaming, dying men and clouds of adobe-brick dust.

There wasn't a man left on his feet in that archway, and no more coming out into it, when Brazos dodged out of the treasure house. Clayburn sprinted across the courtyard after him. They were almost to the door in the wall when a man leaned out of an upper window aiming a rifle down at them.

Brazos and Clayburn fired at the same time. And both bullets struck at the same time. The rifle spilled from the man's hands and bounced on the courtyard below. His torso tilted forward and down and he stayed that way, hanging doubled over the windowsill with his arms dangling.

Clayburn went into the wall after Brazos. Along the passage and up the steps.

On top of the wall, Fenton was down on one knee, firing his rifle at the troopers gathering at the other end of the wall around the watchtower. Most of his bullets hit where he aimed. But there were bullets coming Fenton's way too. And they were coming closer each time.

The instant Juan and Latigo came up out of the inner stairwell, Fenton dropped his rifle. He grabbed the extra pair of loot bags from them, slung the rawhide thong connecting them across the back of his neck, and jumped from the wall to the river below. Juan and Latigo leaped after him, with rifle slugs beating the air around them as they fell.

Brazos emerged on top of the wall an instant later. He got one step across the top—and that was all. Clayburn, coming up behind him, saw the bullet strike the side of Brazos' head, drilling into his skull. He was spun around in a half-turn that gave Clayburn a blurred glimpse of his face. It was already the face of a dead man, before Brazos fell straight forward over the inner edge of the wall to the courtyard below.

Clayburn went across the top of the wall in a crouch, and off the outer edge. He plummeted downward with dizzying speed, feet first. The dark, rushing waters came up to meet him. The weight of the jewel-filled canvas bags tilted him forward and he smacked the surface of the river with his face and the entire length of his body. The solid impact knocked the breath out of him, and he sank under before he could get any air back into his lungs.

The swift-flowing water engulfed him, whirled him around and around. His hip slammed off a submerged rock. Savagely, he fought to get his nose and mouth above water. His empty lungs seemed caught in an agonizing vise; trapped blood hammered at the backs of his eyes, the inside of his skull. With both arms wrapped tightly around the bulky canvas bags he scissored his legs again and again, driving himself up toward the surface.

And then his face was out of the water, his wide-open mouth gulping air. He was already beyond the fortress. There was the booming of cannons and splutter of rifles from the top of the walls. Bullets smacked the surface of the water around him. Fifty yards away a cannonball plunged into the river, sending up a great gusher. Another struck the far bank, bounding high into the air. A waste of ammunition and effort. The small heads bobbing along the night-shrouded surface at great speed and increasing distance made impossible targets.

The strong current sped Clayburn further from the fortress with every second; nearer to the looming mass of the cliff. The surging waters spun him, pulled him downward, flung him up again, battered his head and shoulders. He concentrated all his efforts on getting his face above the surface as often as possible, on holding onto the canvas bags, on keeping to the middle of the foaming torrent. The base of the cliff rushed at him.

And then he was plunging down into the black hole under the cliff. What happened to him there, he could no longer control in the slightest. He was caught within the overwhelming force of a waterfall dragging him through a narrowing stone funnel.

He was engulfed once more by the water that kept sucking him down, down, down. . . . Finally his confused senses registered that the flow of the surrounding water was levelling off. Legs and hands thrashing wildly, he struggled upward. But when his head grazed the stone roof of the funnel, his face was still under water.

The pull of the driving current sucked him down again, his lungs bursting, his eyes bulging out of their sockets. His stomach scraped across the stone bottom as the water dragged him on and on. He kicked hard at the bottom with both feet, driving himself upward in another attempt to break surface.

This time his face bobbed out of the water, into the clear. For a second he was dragging air into his lungs, staring into total, solid darkness so impenetrable that he could not have seen anything an eighth of an inch in front of his eyes. So there was no warning at all. One moment he was taking a great gulp of air and staring into featureless blackness; the next moment his forehead smacked against hard, solid rock.

Something clicked inside his brain, and he was down under the water again, his legs and arms no longer functioning; drowning as he lost consciousness.

NINETEEN

Dietrich set out from the fortress before dawn with forty mounted men.

There was no way of predicting exactly how many rebels would be waiting on the other side of the mountains, where that river flowed out of the caves into an open valley. However, Dietrich was sure of one thing, from the reports of his spies: So far the rebels had not been able to muster more than some twenty men who possessed modern weapons. And Dietrich had double that number with him now. Some of them were his own men. The rest had been Otero's men; now they, too, were his. Anyone who had fought for Otero was hated too much by the people of the country to be safe on his own, even if he wanted to quit.

The route across the mountains was a long, hard, circuitous one. Dietrich did not know if they could reach the exit from the caves before the men who had robbed the treasure house. But he had to try.

He knew all the stories of men in the past who had been carried under the mountains by that river. Most had never been seen again. But one was supposed to have gotten through in less than a day. And the thieves, so well prepared and organized in everything else they had done, would surely have taken some means of obtaining light with them down into those caves. With something to light their way, they might be able to get through much quicker than even the man who'd blundered his way through in a day.

Dietrich pushed his riders hard all the way, allowing them

140

a few hours of rest only when he was certain the men and horses were too exhausted to go on without it. Even so, it took them all that day, and the entire following night, to get across the mountains.

It was late dawn when they rode down into the wide green valley where the river reappeared out of the low mouth of a cave in a rocky, wooded mountain slope. And found no one there.

But someone had *been* there.

The tracks in the soft dirt near the opening where the river gushed out of the mountain told the story plain enough. Eight horses had come here, and been picketed to graze the grass while they waited. There had been two riders with them—one a young boy or a woman, judging by the boot imprints. They had been joined some time later—exactly when could not be judged—by three men who had come from the cave exit, along the river bank.

Three men. That meant that something had happened to one of the four who'd jumped from the fortress wall into the river. But Dietrich drew only a small satisfaction from that; it did not bring that fortune in jewels back.

The three who had gotten through, and the two who'd been waiting for them, had mounted up and ridden across the river. On the other side, the tracks of all eight horses led away up the length of the valley. Wherever they'd gone, they were no longer in sight.

Dietrich mounted up and signaled his men to follow. But he rode up the valley with little hope of catching the ones he was after. The horses of the rebels had had a long rest here before moving on. The horses carrying Dietrich and his men had been pushed to the limit through an entire day and night— and were stumbling with fatigue. . . .

Back inside the dark, low mouth of the cave, Serina crouched behind a hump of knotted limestone and watched them go.

It had been a simple matter to get into the cave without leaving bootprints. She had merely dismounted in the river. Juan Ramirez had tugged her horse the rest of the way across by a lead rope, and led it away with the others. While she had waded against the current in shallow water until she was inside the cave and could climb out of the river.

Now she waited until Dietrich and his men were out of sight at the other end of the valley. Then she struck a match and lit the short, fat candle she held in her hand. With its faint glow showing her the way, she went deeper into the low, narrow cave. After some fifty yards, she turned into a side corridor in the limestone. At the end of this corridor she turned another corner, and the candle shed flickering light in the darkness of a high-domed chamber.

The chamber was about fifty feet wide and a hundred feet long. Fluted columns of pink and white and yellow limestone rose up from the floor of the chamber. From the domed roof more limestone formations hung down, taking the forms of sharp-pointed lances and gracefully flowing draperies. Serina dripped some melting wax on a low hump of rock and anchored the burning candle on it. Then she squatted beside Clayburn.

He lay on the floor of the chamber, stretched out on his back between the hump of rock and a graceful spire whose crystals glistened in the candlelight. Serina watched his face react to the light, the lean muscles around his eyes clenching, then relaxing. She reached out and prodded him with a fingertip.

His eyes blinked open. He stared at her, his eyes slowly focusing. The tip of his tongue moved across his lips. "Serina. . . ."

She smiled at him. "Ah! You know me. Last time you didn't."

"Last time?"

"Don't you remember? You were still unconscious when they brought you here. Then, when I was left alone with you, you came to for awhile—before you fell asleep again. But you didn't know me. And you talked, but you didn't make sense."

Clayburn thought back, but couldn't remember it. "What happened to me?"

"You hit your head. Almost drowned. But Juan Ramirez

got hold of you, pulled you out in time. You were still holding onto the jewel bags.''

Clayburn remembered then. With difficulty, he pushed up on one elbow. He felt weak, slightly dizzy. And his forehead was sore. But it didn't hurt inside. Apparently he'd slept off the headache.

He looked around him, then back to Serina as he suddenly realized what her being here with him meant. ''We got through. . . .''

Serina nodded. ''In less than ten hours. With the candles to light the way, it was not difficult. There was steam coming from cracks in the bottom of the caves. All they had to do part of the way was to follow where the air currents took the steam. Of course, it was not easy. They had to crawl and climb and. . . .''

''*They* crawled and climbed,'' Clayburn interrupted. ''How did I make it?''

''They carried you. My brother and Fenton.'' Serina's face darkened with anger. ''Juan Ramirez dried and cleaned his gun as soon as you were out of the water—and then turned on my brother and Fenton, and made them give up their guns to him. Then he forced them to go ahead of him, carrying you.''

Clayburn smiled a little. ''Juan always was bright—even as a kid.''

''You don't trust my brother either?'' Serina snapped indignantly. ''You think he would steal the jewels? He is working for something much more important than that.''

''Maybe. . . . But what about Fenton? You really trust him that much?''

She thought about it. ''No. . . . Perhaps not. He is not like Gila, for whom my brother is a god.''

Clayburn let that go by. ''So we all got through. . . .''

''Except Brazos Williams. He was killed.''

''I know.''

''It doesn't matter,'' Serina said. ''There were enough jewels in what you did bring through to pay for the rifles and ammunition.'' Then she saw the way he was looking at her, and paused. When she spoke again, her voice was low: "Brazos was a friend of yours, too?"

"Yes."

Serina heaved a sigh. "I'm sorry. . . . Now you will hate me."

"Why? *You* didn't kill him."

Serina told him the rest of it. How when they'd come out of the caves, Juan had disarmed Gila before he realized what Juan intended. How they had ridden on with all the horses, leaving her here to tend Clayburn. When they got a good distance from here, on solid rock where they would leave no trail to follow, Juan would separate from the others. He'd leave their guns behind when he was far enough away from them to be safe—and continue north with the jewels to exchange them for the arms and ammunition.

Latigo, Fenton and Gila would circle back here in a few days to pick up Serina and Clayburn. Then they'd go on to Oputo to await word from Juan Ramirez.

Serina told Clayburn about seeing Dietrich and his men; and then she turned to her saddlebags which lay on the ground beside her. "Juan said to give this to you when you awoke."

It was Clayburn's knife. Juan had retrieved it for him. Remembering where he had left it, Clayburn put the knife beside him. He laid his head down and shut his eyes. Made his mind blank and sank back into sleep. . . .

When he awoke again it was to the smell of coffee and beans. He opened his eyes and saw Serina a few feet away in front of a small fire of burning twigs.

He sat up, slowly, testing himself. But he was surprised to find that he didn't feel bad at all any more, except for the soreness of various bruises. Serina turned her head and saw him.

"Good morning," she said mockingly, and turned back to her fire. Pouring coffee into two tin cups, she handed him one.

He nodded his thanks as he took it. "All the comforts of home."

"We will be here for three days, waiting for them to come

back for us. We have to eat." She got him a tin plate of hot beans and a couple of strips of jerked beef.

They both ate hungrily. By the time they were finished, the twigs had burned out, leaving only the light of the candle inside the domed chamber. Clayburn washed down the meal with the last of the coffee, sighed with satisfaction as he put down the tin cup.

Serina eyed him. "You feel better now."

"Much."

"Because I took good care of you." Her eyes laughed at him, but there was a sultry guile behind the laughter. "You should thank me."

He did what she wanted, taking her shoulders in his hands and pulling her to him. When he finished kissing her, her eyes were almost closed and her head tilted back limply.

"Are you sure," she whispered, "that you won't change your mind about helping my brother?"

His smile mocked her. "Quite sure. . . . Another thing I'm sure of is that I'll never wind up rich and respectable. And that's what you want, remember?"

She sighed, deep in her throat. "That is what I want. For a husband. And that is what I'll get—sooner or later." Her dark eyes opened a bit more, looking into his. "But in the meantime," she said softly, "we have three days to wait here together. With nothing else to do. . . ."

Her lips pursed as though for another kiss. She turned away from him, and blew out the candle. And then she turned back to him in the darkness, and her mouth was hungry and demanding on his.

Dietrich lost the tracks of the eight horses he was trailing in a maze of stone canyons shortly before dusk. And did not find them again the next day. As he turned back with his forty soldiers toward the fortress, he kept pondering on the wealth that had been looted from the fortress.

And Captain Cullen—or the man who'd called himself that. It didn't matter to Dietrich, now, who he really was. Only one thing was important: Were he and the others who'd been with him merely thieves—or were they with Juan Ramirez?

He learned the answer on reaching the fortress. Hogan had returned the previous day, along with the other man he'd sent back north. It was the other man who'd heard that Juan Ramirez had been seen in Bisbee. Dietrich had sent them both back to Bisbee to find out what Ramirez had been doing there.

And they *had* found out. Juan Ramirez had made contact with a man there, to arrange for the delivery of a large shipment of modern Winchester repeating rifles, plus ammunition. But that was all they could learn. The man Ramirez had contacted had vanished from Bisbee by the time they got there. And no one knew where, when or how the arms would be delivered to Ramirez.

That left no doubt in Dietrich's mind. The loot from the fortress had gone north—to enable Juan Ramirez to arm the people of this country for a full-scale rebellion.

And before Dietrich could do anything about it, he would need information. There was only one way to obtain it: An hour after his talk with Hogan and the other man, he was sending out word to the spies Otero had managed to plant among the people. From now on they were to forget everything else, and concentrate on worming their way into the confidences of anyone likely to go off to join the rebel force when those arms arrived. . . .

Then Dietrich settled down to wait.

He waited for three weeks. And then one of the spies arrived at the fortress with what Dietrich had been waiting for. The spy had managed to join a small group of men from his village who'd gone up into the mountains to hide and wait for orders from the rebel leader. Those orders had finally arrived—calling on them to go to Oputo. Juan Ramirez and the newly-purchased arms would arrive in Oputo within the next two days.

Dietrich digested this news slowly, standing in the middle of his headquarters office and staring bleakly at the map on the wall. He had much to win—or lose. He had spent his life fighting other men's wars for them. But this one he had managed to make his own.

With Otero dead, his position had fallen on the shoulders

of his second-in-command, Captain Sanchez. And Sanchez had become Dietrich's man even before Otero had died. Now Sanchez officially ruled here. But Dietrich ruled Sanchez. The part of Sonora over which Otero had gained control belonged to Dietrich now—if he could hold it. Holding a country of rebellious, well-armed people, Dietrich knew from experience, was an almost impossible job.

But they were *not* well-armed—not quite yet. The time to move in force against the rebels was now—immediately— before Juan Ramirez could finish distributing those Winchesters among the people, and training them how to use them properly. If he struck at Oputo, swiftly and by surprise, he could tear the heart out of the rebellion before it began.

Dietrich strode from his office and began issuing his orders in a cold, controlled voice. An hour later he was riding out of the fortress at the head of two hundred men, headed toward Oputo.

TWENTY

Taut-nerved, Clayburn waited on one knee behind a screen of junipers on the south slope of the heavily-wooded mountain pass. All along the slope other men were waiting, hidden behind trees, rocks, hollows, bushes.

There were more men concealed along the opposite slope, where Juan Ramirez had his command post. And still more around the bend in the west end pass, where Latigo was in charge. With Latigo were Fenton, Gila and several more of his gang. But most were like those along the slopes; men of a different breed. Farmers, ranchers, vaqueros, shepherds, townsmen. . . . Men with hate twisting their guts and Winchester repeating rifles in their fists. More than enough men to get the job done, if they only held fire as Juan had hammered it into them they must.

The east end of the pass was open. That was the way Dietrich was coming. The only way to get a large body of riders through to the town of Oputo, nestled deep inside these mountains. The dust of their coming was already in sight, rising in the distance.

It had been Juan's plan, from start to finish. He'd planned it this way even before he'd gone north to make a deal for those Winchesters. The arms and ammunition had been brought down to a secret hideout in a box canyon over a week ago. Nearly three hundred rebels had been gathered into that box canyon, and kept there almost as prisoners. The way out had been sealed off and carefully guarded, so that no spy among them could possibly slip out. For a full week the small number of men who were expert in the use of the Winchesters had trained the larger number who were not. Then Juan had sent out word for any other rebels in the country to come to Oputo and wait for arms to arrive—knowing news of it was bound to trickle to one of Dietrich's informers. After that, all they had to do was hide themselves in this pass, and wait.

Clayburn waited. Watching the wooded bottom of the pass through the juniper boughs that concealed him. Fingering the carbine he held ready.

Two Dietrich outriders came through the trees below, scouting the way ahead through the pass. They went by, hearing nothing and seeing nothing. As they turned the bend they saw the barricade of rocks and logs stretched across the west end of the pass dead ahead of them, blocking the way. But neither had a chance to react. Two men dropped from the overhead tree-branches and landed on top of them, knocking them from their horses. By the time Dietrich's scouts hit the ground, each had a knife in his heart.

Ten minutes later Dietrich came through the pass, riding beside Captain Sanchez at the head of his army.

Clayburn took aim at Dietrich—and just managed to check himself, keeping his trigger-finger from squeezing only by a jolt of intense control. No one was to fire until Juan gave the signal. Clayburn had sworn to abide by this, along with the others.

His face wooden, he kept Dietrich in his sights as long as he could. But Dietrich vanished into the timber down near the bend before the last of his troops came into the pass, under the hidden guns.

Juan's single rifle-shot cracked from the opposite slope. An invisible hand seemed to slap one of the troopers below out of his saddle. Clayburn instantly switched aim and squeezed the trigger, spilling another trooper backwards off his mount. At the same time every other rifle along both slopes let go with a deafening, point-blank volley that smashed into the stunned double column of riders below. Both columns shredded apart as men and horses went down under a continuing, concentrated barrage from both sides of them. Men who survived the first few seconds broke out of their shock and grabbed for their weapons; their senses reel-

ing as they found themselves engulfed in a volcano of gunfire
and screaming and flailing bits of lead.

At the head of his ambushed army, Dietrich had reacted
instantly, instinctively. Raking his horse with his spurs and
charging forward around the bend—signalling and yelling for
his men to follow; hearing the pound of horses behind him
as those nearest to him obeyed.

He raced through the trees around the bend—and saw the
barricade blocking the way ahead. Again his response was
immediate, with no need for thought. He yanked the reins,
wheeling his mount completely around; racing back into the
heavier timber as the riflemen behind the barricade loosed a
thundering volley.

Bullets whipped the air on both sides of him, tugging at
his sleeve, tearing the hat from his head. He saw Captain
Sanchez directly ahead of him tilt sideways from his saddle,
a pistol still gripped in his hand, his face a welter of blood
and broken bones. Two other men were shot from their saddles at the same time. To Dietrich's right, a horse went down
crushing its rider under it. And then Dietrich's horse staggered under him and fell.

Dietrich kicked clear as it dropped, landed on his feet, and
sprinted to Captain Sanchez's horse.

Latigo, sitting his horse at one end of the barricade, saw
the blond, hatless man reach the horse—and recognized him
in the split-second before Dietrich grabbed the reins and
pulled the horse after him behind a thick screen of high
bushes. With an exultant yell, Latigo kicked his horse forward, the Colt in his right fist coming up.

Dietrich was swinging into the saddle when Latigo came
crashing through the bushes at him, firing the Colt. The first
shot missed. Shooting from a moving horse didn't make for
accuracy. Dietrich did not go for his own holstered gun.
Instead he whipped the officer's saber from the saddle scabbard and swung it in a long, looping arc as he wheeled his
mount into Latigo's.

The collision of the two horses made Latigo's second shot
miss too, by a fraction of an inch. Dietrich's saber did not
miss. The long, curved steel slashed into Latigo's side just

below the ribs, cutting in so deep that the hilt was pulled
from Dietrich's grasp as Latigo fell out of the saddle.

Latigo hit the ground on his hands and knees. He stayed
that way for a moment, his face contorted with agony. Then
he shoved slowly to his feet, both hands closing on the hilt
of the saber embedded in him. He took three staggering steps
through the bushes toward the barricade before his eyes went
dead and he sank back to the ground.

Gila saw him. And leaped the barricade, running toward
him. He was almost there when a bullet broke his spine.

Fenton saw, too. He slipped from his horse, and sat down
behind the barricade where he'd be safe. There was no point
in risking his skin anymore. Latigo had decided to be a
hero—and wasn't going to be a big man down here after all.
He'd have done better to concentrate on making a more determined try for the jewelry, as he'd originally planned. . . .

Dietrich, racing back around the bend to rally his men,
found that it was too late for that. What survived of his army
was too scattered, milling in all directions under a continuing
hail of rifle bullets. There were a few pockets of resistance.
Small groups of his men crouched behind timber in the floor
of the pass, firing back up at the slopes. But not enough of
them to count.

Most of them were fleeing in panic—back through the pass;
up the slopes. Some would get out; but again, not enough to
count. Dietrich made his decision as soon as he grasped the
hopelessness of the situation. He'd been in enough battles to
know that this one was already lost. And with the battle, he
had lost the war, and this country.

The only alternatives left were to gather as many of his
survivors as he could for a doomed, last-ditch defense—or
escape. Dietrich elected for escape. There would be other
wars, in other countries.

To attempt to ride back through the pass would mean running the gauntlet of the entire length of both lines of hidden
riflemen on the slopes. That would be suicide. The numbers
of riderless horses and dying men down at that end proved it.

The south slope would be the easier climb. But the north
slope, though steeper, was more densely wooded. Dietrich

crouched low over the neck of his horse and kicked it toward the north slope.

He was into the sparse lower timber on the slope when Clayburn took aim from the opposite slope. It was too far, Dietrich was moving too fast, and the leafed branches of the trees obscured the target. Clayburn's shot killed the horse under Dietrich.

He saw Dietrich fall behind the body of the horse. He waited, but Dietrich did not reappear. Pushing through the junipers, Clayburn started running down the south slope toward the bottom. . . .

Stretched out full length behind the cover of the dead horse, Dietrich raised his head cautiously for a swift look at what there was around him. He was in a sparse grove of small, thin pines. The thicker timber was further up the slope, some distance above him. Something caught his eye. A dead man sprawled under a bush ten feet away. One of his own men. Something else caught his attention: a slight movement behind a tree. He was watching this tree when he heard the pounding of a horse coming up the slope.

Dietrich turned his head just in time to see Hogan ride past him, racing the horse up toward the thicker timber.

Juan Ramirez stepped out from behind the tree Dietrich had been watching, just as Hogan reached it. Hogan swiveled in his saddle, bringing around the gun in his fist as Juan brought up the one in his.

It was Juan's gun that roared first. The heavy lead slug smashed through Hogan's teeth and went up through the roof of his mouth into his brain. Hogan's gun went off as he fell, the bullet chopping into the dirt at Juan's feet. The riderless horse skittered away in terror—toward Dietrich. It came to an uncertain halt only ten feet from him.

Dietrich drew his gun and raised up another inch—just enough to take aim at Juan without exposing anything of himself to shoot at. Juan caught the flash of movement from the corner of his eye and dodged back behind the tree. He almost made it. Most of him was behind the trunk of the tree when Dietrich fired at the part of him he could still see. The bullet drilled into Juan's leg, breaking bone.

Juan toppled, hitting the ground hard, losing his gun. Dietrich sprang up and sprinted for Hogan's horse, caught it and went up into the saddle. Juan fumbled blindly for his fallen gun, his vision fogged with the pain. His fingers finally closed on it. He rubbed his eyes viciously with the heel of his other hand, hearing the sounds of a horse racing away up the slope.

His vision cleared in time for him to see Dietrich ride into the heavy timber at the top of the slope. Not in time to take aim before Dietrich vanished from sight.

Juan put down the gun and began to curse through his pain-clenched teeth. He tore the bandanna from his neck and tied it tightly around his leg, above the wound, as a tourniquet. Picking up the gun, he slid the barrel between the knotted bandanna and the leg, began using it to twist the bandanna tighter and stop the flow of blood.

The gunfire in the pass was dying out when Clayburn came up the slope to him. Clayburn paused just long enough to make sure the wound wasn't anything Juan couldn't handle himself until one of the others got to him.

Then he scanned the surrounding area. "Where is he?"

Juan's pain-covered eyes looked up the slope, and he pointed to the spot where he had last seen Dietrich. "Mounted. . . ." he said through his teeth. "He's all yours. . . ."

There was no need for either to explain who they were talking about. Clayburn went looking for a horse.

It was late afternoon when Dietrich came to a stream rushing down a fold in the mountains. He drew rein and looked back. He had come a long way, and still there was no sign of pursuit.

Kneeing the horse forward into the stream, he drew rein again in the middle of it. By staying in the water as far as he could, he would leave no tracks for anyone to follow. The logical and easiest way was to go downstream; the slope was steep and the force of the current very strong. Dietrich dismounted and started upstream, against the current, dragging the horse up after him.

He stayed with the stream until a waterfall blocked his way. Here the left bank of the stream was smooth stone, rising gently, leveling off into a narrow stone gully. The right bank was under an eroded cliff, and it was choked with rock rubble. The wet tracks he would make on either side would soon dry away and vanish; and the right bank would be much harder going. Dietrich went to the right.

It *was* hard going. It took him nearly half an hour to get over the rock rubble, into a low, stone-floored ravine. He followed the ravine for an hour. It was dusk when the ravine opened into a wide, sheer-walled canyon.

Dietrich rode down the length of the canyon and turned off it into the first break in the walls he came to: another ravine, this one deep and narrow. By nightfall it had widened considerably, into an area of stone spires and buttes and boulders. There Dietrich finally came to a halt. Both he and the horse were exhausted. And to try moving further through the darkness would be to risk the horse breaking a leg.

Hobbling the horse beside one of the boulders, he stripped the saddle from it and searched in Hogan's saddlebags. He found the food supplies he was looking for, but he could not eat much. And when he stretched out on the ground he found it hard to fall asleep, despite his fatigue.

It wasn't fear of pursuit. No one could possibly have followed him this far. Not unless the pursuer could read his mind. He had changed direction too often, wherever he would leave no trail that anyone but an Indian could find; each time choosing the more unlikely route.

It was the knowledge of what he had almost won for himself in this country that kept jagging at his mind. And the shocking suddenness with which it had all been lost. Vivid memories of the disaster in the pass kept going through his brain.

Finally his thoughts became a whirling blur, merging into dreams. . . .

The sun had been up for two hours when he woke suddenly, with a nerve-plucking sense of something wrong. He drew his gun as he came to his feet, looking around him warily. There was nothing to be seen but the buttes and spires and boulders—and he realized that what had disturbed him was the realization that he'd overslept.

Holstering his Colt, he walked toward his hobbled horse.

He was reaching down for the saddle beside the boulder when a soft voice behind him said: "Dietrich. . . ."

He froze in position for a moment. His hands were empty, but the right one was only inches from the holstered gun. . . .

He straightened without reaching for it. There was a thin, hard smile to his mouth and his eyes had an opaque gloss to them when he turned around and saw Clayburn standing there beside one of the stone spires.

"It would be you," Dietrich said quietly.

"Yes." The gun in Clayburn's hand was steady on a point in the exact center of Dietrich's chest. His nostrils were pinched and his mouth was sullen.

"Why?" Dietrich asked. "What have you to do with these rebels?"

"Nothing." Clayburn's voice was toneless. "But you hung a man named Diego Ramirez."

Dietrich's eyed widened just a bit. All of him was concentrated on the right hand that was waiting for a chance to reach for the holstered gun. "He was a friend?"

"More than that."

"I see. . . ." Dietrich said. What was in the depths of Clayburn's eyes made him choose his words slowly, with care: "You have come for revenge. To challenge me. . . . All right; this is as good a time and place as any. All you have to do is holster your gun and. . . ."

"I didn't come to fight you," Clayburn told him evenly. "I came to kill you."

The gun in his hand made a sharp, harsh noise in the confines of the ravine.

Dietrich fell back against the boulder, both hands clutching at the blood-welling hole in his chest. He stared at Clayburn with shocked disbelief. Slowly, he slid down to his knees and toppled over on his side, both hands still pressing hard at the wound, trying to stop the blood from flowing out of him.

Clayburn stood over him, looking down. Dietrich's breathing became a harsh, desperate struggle to hold onto his ebbing life. Clayburn stayed there, watching him; waiting.

Dietrich was a long time dying. Clayburn did not turn away and leave until he was finished.

About the Author

Marvin H. Albert was born in Philadelphia and has lived in New York, Los Angeles, London, Rome, and Paris. He currently lives on the Riviera with his wife, the French artist Xenia Klar. He has two children, Jan and David.

He has been a Merchant Marine Officer, actor and theatrical road manager, newspaperman, magazine editor, and Hollywood script writer, in addition to being the author of numerous books of fiction and nonfiction.

Several of his books have been Literary Guild choices. He has been honored with a Special Award by the Mystery Writers of America. Nine of his novels have been made into motion pictures.